Deadly GAMES

USA Today Bestselling Author
Khardine Gray
writing as
Faith Summers

DEADLY GAMES

A DARK MAFIA ROMANCE

KHARDINE GRAY
FAITH SUMMERS

DARK ROMANCE NOTE

AUTHOR NOTE

Please note Faith Summers is the Dark romance pen name of USA Today Bestselling Author Khardine Gray

ALSO BY FAITH SUMMERS

Faith Summers Collection

Series

Dark Syndicate

Ruthless Prince

Dark Captor

Wicked Liar

Merciless Hunter

Heartless Lover

Ruthless King

Dark Odyssey

Tease Me

Taunt Me

Thrill Me

Tempt Me

Take Me

Original Sins

Deal with the Beast

Theirs

PLAYLIST

1. Touch Me -Dj Rui Da Silva-
2. Hollow- Four Star Mary
3. Here with Me- Dido
4. Always- Bon Jovi
5. Darkness- Eminem
6. Thinking Out Loud - Ed Sheeran
7. My Immortal - Evanescence
8. The Only Exception- Paramore
9. Complicated- Avril Lavigne
10. Four Star Mary- Fate
11. Crazy- Aerosmith -

12. When You're Gone -The Cranberries

13. Fearless- Goo Goo Dolls

14. Torn- Natalia Imbruglia

15. Dilate- Four Star Mary

16. Wherever You Will Go- The Calling

Check out the playlist on spotify xx

WE WERE SUPPOSED TO BE TWO PASSING SHIPS ON AN UNFORGETTABLE NIGHT...

I accepted a foolish dare that changed everything–
pretend you're someone you aren't until sunrise.

I chose to be normal and free.
Not bound by the duties my father forced on me.

The sinfully gorgeous god-like man staring at me in the club with the I'm-going-to-devour-you smile was who I picked to be *normal and free* with.

It didn't matter that he looked like the kind of villain I should run from.

Mercilessly, he claimed my virtue.
And something I never knew existed until him.

That was supposed to be it.

One night. One time. One fantasy.

At sunrise, we'd go our separate ways.

Except, I never knew my one-night stand would turn out to be my father's new bodyguard.
Or... that he isn't who he says he is.

Not only does Lukiyan Romanechka have dark secrets and a separate agenda that's about to fuel a war, but there's also something else he wants.
Me...

Like Hades, he wants to steal me away from the light and take me to his dark world.

And I just might let him.

Deadly Games is a dark mafia romance inspired by Hades & Persephone's story. It contains dubious situations, mature content, and graphic violence some readers might find offensive and/or triggering.

This is a complete STANDALONE in the Dark Syndicate world.

PROLOGUE

Lukiyan

Fate or coincidence...

Sometimes I believe they are one and the same, but then the Universe corrects me and shows me they aren't.

The night I met her was an example of that.

It had to be.

I refuse to believe the circumstances which led me to Persephone Vittorio could have been anything close to a coincidence.

When I first saw her, I was instantly in love.

I just never realized love had infected me until it dug its claws into my heart and ripped it from my chest, showing living proof that I'm still human.

At that moment, I understood perfectly why Hades did what he did.

So when my Persephone danced her way into my life, I decided she had to be mine, no matter the cost.

No matter the sacrifice.

No matter that stealing her from the light meant pulling her into my world of , death and darkness.

She was always going to be mine to keep.

Mine always.

Mine, whether she wanted to be or not....

PERSEPHONE

Sao Paulo, Brazil
Three months ago

"I'm going to fuck you," my handsome stranger husks in my ear.

His voice is a deep baritone that bewitched me from the first moment I heard him speak.

The thought of him ripping off my clothes and fucking me sends a jolt of undiluted desire straight to my brain.

I can't talk. Anything I might have thought to say fades from my mind when his delicious lips crush against mine again. The effect is like gasoline being poured over fire.

Explosive waves of pleasure crash into my soul, paralyzing my body.

His kiss is cruel and overwhelming, sending scorching

shivers of raw arousal from the top of my head to the tips of my toes.

He kicks the door open without taking his lips from mine, and we fall into his bedroom, our bodies crashing against the wall. Moisture beads between my thighs when he presses me into the hard surface, and his massive erection pushes against my belly.

As he continues to consume my mouth, my insides melt, succumbing to the desire spiking my nerves. I surrender completely, my mind falling into a whirlpool of lust, my body bowing to the delicious assault on my lips.

Oh my God... I can't believe I'm going to do this.

I'm really going to do this.

Something wild and reckless and forbidden.

I'm going to fuck the sexy-as-hell man I just met in a club.

I don't even know his name. And he doesn't know mine.

He is all I'm aware of and all I want to think of right now.

Mr. Gorgeous—the tall, *tall*, dark blond, god-like man with a face that looks like it was carved to perfection by an angel. Decadent tattoos cover his neck and forearms in a tasteful, well-thought-out manner, making me think he's a man who appreciates art.

His body feels like it was cut from granite, and there's an untamed vibe about his entire presence that beckons me to obey his every command.

Everything about him is raw and masculine, sexy and wild.

Dangerous.

I know danger when I see it. When you're born into the mafia, you eat, sleep, and live around danger.

Although I haven't been able to figure him out, I knew he was dangerous the instant I saw him watching me dance from afar. I knew, and still I entertained this.

When he asked me to go home with him, I agreed. Now I'm here.

Here in this house where nobody who has power over me knows where I am.

I'm free—*for now.*

And this is me being me. Not the buzz from the triple shot of vodka the bartender added to my kamikaze cocktail back at the club.

This is *all* me, being who I would be if my life belonged to me.

Pretend to be someone you're not until sunrise.

That is the unsolicited advice I decided to take from a carnival-themed fortune cookie I picked up yesterday at one of the stalls on the beach. When I opened the cookie and read the little note, it was like the Universe was screaming at me, handing me a momentary fix.

So tonight, I'm pretending to be the version of myself I've always wanted to be.

Given my past and who I am, I might be foolish for following such craziness. However, after the fucking bomb my father dropped on me earlier, *nothing* felt more appealing than pretending I wasn't living in a world where my life had crumbled and gone to shit.

In my desperation to stop myself from going insane, I accepted the dare and I'm glad I did.

Mr. Gorgeous will be the first man to have me and I don't care that this is reckless and crazy, because he's my choice.

And tonight I'm choosing to give my body to him.

On what remains of my twenty-first birthday, I owe it to my borrowed life to live for one night doing what I want.

After all, there was a time in my life when I was told I wouldn't make it past eighteen.

With that reasoning, I run my fingers through the spiky strands of my handsome stranger's hair and savor the pleasure of touching him.

I get lost in the way he claims my mouth and holds me like he wants to consume me.

Until he catches my face in a deathlike grip, and I'm swiftly pulled from my reverie.

He stops kissing me and presses his fingers into my neck, tightening his grip.

I gasp, feeling certain he could snap it, as if I were little more than a twig in the confines of his strength.

He shocks me further when he tugs at the waist of my little dress and rips it right off my body, leaving me in just my strapless bra, my panties, and my ballet pumps.

A villainous smile lifts the corners of his lips. I shudder under the weight of his hungry stare, which morphs into curiosity the moment his gaze lands on the tattoo on my chest.

His eyes lingers there, and he stares at the beautiful design of little pink roses and blue butterflies resting on the larger petals.

I already know he's looking at it with such interest because it doesn't suit me.

I agree. Although I love tattoos, I never planned to get one.

My sister was more into tattoos than me. People say twins share all sorts of similarities, but Athena and I couldn't have been more different. Of the two of us, I'm the dainty and delicate sister. I almost think he knows this, even though he doesn't know I had a twin.

Maybe he can guess, though—*that the tattoo isn't really me*—given the rest of my body is bare and the little tattoo is nestled between my cleavage and just big enough so you can only see it when I'm naked or wearing certain clothes. The dress I was wearing wasn't one that exposed it.

I just hope he can't see the remnants of the scar beneath. I don't want to have to explain the whys and whats of how it came to be. The hidden scar which resulted from that runs much deeper and darker than anything visible to the human eye.

His sensual lips part as if he's going to say something, but he doesn't.

Instead, his gaze drops to my breasts, and the breath burning my lungs leaves me when he snaps open the butterfly clasp of my bra.

As my breasts spill out, I become very aware that he's the first man who isn't a doctor to see me like this—*this naked*.

I've never felt more vulnerable, and the wariness I previously felt returns. It only eases when a twinkle enters his eyes, and he looks at me as if I'm the most beautiful woman he's ever seen.

I know that can't be true, but he makes me think it could be.

Filling his palms with my breasts, he tweaks my nipples playfully with his tattooed fingers, sending my body into overdrive. Then he lowers his mouth to my neck and licks the skin right up to my earlobe.

There he lingers as his warm breath whispers over my skin, heating my body up all over again.

"Are you scared of me, Princess?"

"No..." It's a lie, and we both know it. Of course, I'm fucking scared. "Should... I be?"

"That depends. Nice girls like you are usually scared of men like me."

There's that air of danger again.

When my breath hitches, his smile widens. It's as devastatingly disarming as his Mediterranean blue eyes.

Both freeze me in place, and I think of all the reasons why this idea of mine is risky as fuck.

The normal version of myself would never dream of having a one-night stand with a stranger. Not with my adept knowledge of *bad men*.

I'm still trying to figure out which type he is.

He looks like the kind of mafia men from the Camorra I'm used to, but nothing is giving him away. He also speaks American English like me, which makes me think he could be here in Brazil on vacation as well.

The only thing lurking between his words is the lust enticing me to breathe him in.

Seeing my contemplation, he reaches for a lock of my brown hair and takes it between his thumb and forefinger, allowing the ends to curl then loosen.

I'm not sure what fascinates him more—my fear or me. I'm here at his mercy, and he knows it.

I suck in a breath when his clever fingers run down to my pussy, and he rubs my clit through the lace fabric of my panties. In response I moan, unable to restrain myself.

God, that feels so good.

Greedy for his touch, I widen my legs, and he gives me a knowing smile.

"You like that, Princess?" He nibbles on my ear.

"Yes."

He rubs harder, stealing the air from my lungs. "Do you want more?"

I open my mouth, but no words come.

"Answer me."

"Ye...sss."

On my word, he cups my sex and slides the fabric away from my mound so he can slip a finger into my pussy.

The burst of pleasure that lances through me is too much. It's so overwhelming that I have to grip his shirt to stop myself from falling over. But I loosen my grasp when he pulls out and licks my glistening juices off his finger.

"So wet and ready for me," he husks.

I don't think I've ever seen anything more fascinating than watching him taste me.

The smile returns to his handsome face, and he plunges his finger back into my pussy once more, but only to pull out again and place the tip on my lips.

Pushing into my mouth, he makes me taste my arousal, encouraging me to suck his finger.

I do, and it's the hottest thing ever. I suck on the thick skin, watching his eyes darken to the angry blue of the sky in a tempestuous storm. Then suddenly, his coolness slips, and lust seems to take over. At that moment, he tears my panties off the same way he ripped off my dress.

Two thick fingers then plunge into my pussy, sending me reeling in ecstasy as he starts finger-fucking me.

"You, Princess, are one interesting creature."

"Why?" I moan, gripping his shirt, feeling the hard cut of his muscles beneath my fingers.

"Because you have my undivided attention even though you won't tell me your name." His seductive voice pours over me as I moan louder, coming undone in his arms. "Or where you're from."

He stares me down with such intensity it weakens my knees.

It's not that I wouldn't love to tell him my name or where I'm from.

I just can't.

It's safer this way for both of us.

I'm not supposed to be here with him, and he's not supposed to know me.

"I wonder what else you could be hiding in that pretty little head of yours," he adds.

I was relieved earlier when he didn't question me on my identity. Since people have no-name hookups all the time, I thought I might have gotten away with it. I'm still trying to, but perhaps it's not the wisest thing to hide the fact that I'm a virgin.

"I've... never done this before."

"A virgin?" He looks me over again with an incredulous expression.

"Yes," I stutter.

"Well, Princess... that just means I have the pleasure of teaching you how to please me before you get the hard, dirty fuck I plan to give you." His voice is husky with intoxicating sexual greed. "You can start with sucking my dick."

Lust gathers at the back of my throat, and my temperature spikes as my eyes go straight to the bulge pressing against his pants.

I barely get a moment to think before he undoes his belt buckle and shoves his pants down his hips, releasing his thick, long cock. The bulbous head already has pre-cum glistening on the tip.

"Get on your knees." Placing his hand on my head, he forces me to the ground, and like an obedient servant, I obey.

The moment my knees settle on the cool concrete floor, his fingers lace through my hair, and he guides his cock into my mouth.

"Good girl. Now suck." He shoves deeper into my throat as I run my tongue along his shaft. "Harder."

I obey, and he thrusts even deeper, making me gag, but the exhilaration of having his cock in my mouth entices me to do whatever he wants me to do.

"Good girl," he groans, fisting my hair so he can angle my face to take his thrusts. "You're my perfect little slut."

He tweaks my nipples and starts fucking my face, his hips moving wildly, his grip tightening in my hair and the nape of my neck as he pounds mercilessly into my mouth.

Everything becomes wild with the surge of sexual energy rippling between us, and I commit this moment to memory, mentally wiping away all the unsavory encounters I've had with that devil my father practically sold me to.

Mr. Gorgeous pounds harder, and my pussy aches for him to touch me there.

The ache is so intense I find myself rubbing my clit in a desperate attempt to soothe the need.

When he sees me touching myself, his cock twitches, growing harder in my mouth.

"That's my job." Suddenly he pulls his cock out of my mouth and secures a firm grip around my arm, lifting me to stand. "I think it's time I own your greedy pussy."

This is it. The moment I change forever.

I won't be the same Persephone I was when I woke this morning.

I won't be the same girl I was mere hours ago before the world changed and my dreams were taken away from me.

He yanks his shirt off, revealing the granite muscles I fantasized about, and I find myself lost in him again.

His body is a work of art. It's covered in tattoos artistically designed to enhance his sculpted muscles.

There are a series of Japanese characters lining the right and left sides of his abs and an eagle at the base of his hip. The design that catches my eye the most, however, is on his arm. It's a female harlequin clown that looks like it came straight out of a Batman film.

While I openly ogle him, he reaches into his back pocket, takes out a condom, and tears the wrapper. I continue to watch with fascination as he rolls the condom onto his cock.

Pressing me against the wall, he lifts my leg and secures it around his waist. Then he guides his cock to my entrance.

I flinch when he pushes into my pussy, and look away, gasping for air when he forces his way into me.

He grabs my face again, rougher this time, turning me back to meet those eyes of his which now look like shimmers on the sea.

"Look at me while I fuck you."

"Oh… God."

One hard thrust takes him deeper. Another tears right

through my maidenhead and sends a rush of undiluted pleasure through my being as if someone added a dose of napalm to my body.

I cry out from the impact, tightening my grip on him. He holds me too, and begins moving inside me, pumping slowly at first, then faster and faster, until he builds up a steady rhythm that holds me in ultimate ecstasy.

My body comes alive with erotic bliss, luxuriating in the sensation.

Then he speeds up and starts fucking me relentlessly into the wall.

He pounds into my body over and over again, taking me higher out of this world.

It hurts. He's hurting me so damn much, but I'm so aroused that pleasure and pain feel like the same sweet, delicious thing.

My head spins, and desire rides the wave of arousal racing up and down my spine while he continues to claim me with the skill of a man who knows what he's doing. And what I need.

The first wave of a fierce orgasm tugs savagely at my insides, making the walls of my pussy spasm around his cock. Then I come, and it's like nothing I've ever experienced.

Pleasure explodes from the depths of my soul, forcing mindless moans from my lips. My cries of ecstasy join the erotic melody of our bodies slapping together.

One hand squeezes my hip and the other grips my neck as he tilts my face up to kiss me again.

"You're mine now. All mine," he growls, picking me up.

I wrap my legs around his waist as he continues plunging into my body like a savage.

We collapse on the king-size bed in the center of the room. There he pulls out briefly to flip me onto my hands and knees.

"This ass is mine," he declares, giving my cheek a hard smack that jolts my body.

I cry out from the sting, and before I can get over the shock of what he just did, he spanks me again and again.

The maddening sensation of incongruent pleasure assaults my body, leaving me delirious and utterly stunned by the new arousal coiling through me.

Another smack on my raw skin has me panting like a dog.

Then he shocks me further when he runs his tongue right over the tight rosette of my asshole and licks across the searing heat of my ass cheeks where he spanked me.

Despite the frenzy of arousal and pain racing through me, my entire being goes tense when I feel the head of his cock pushing into my asshole.

"Now it's time to make you scream," he declares. "I'm owning you here, too."

I don't get the chance to process what he's about to do because he just does it, pushing his hard cock deeper into my ass until he's all the way in.

Instantly I scream as if programmed to do so when the burning sensation ravages my body.

Fuck! It fucking hurts so much that stars speckle my vision.

"It… hurts," I choke out weakly.

"Then *red* is your safe word. Say it, Princess… and I stop."

The pain is so unbearable I'm grateful for the offer, but when I open my mouth to say *red,* nothing comes out of me but a whimper of pleasure.

Mr. Gorgeous prods at my ass, sliding in and out slowly. Tortuously *slowly,* and purposefully.

All I hear next is the deep rumble of his laughter.

"Bad girl. I knew you wouldn't say it. You like it dark and dirty, don't you?" He pushes in harder. "You like the thought of me owning every part of your body."

I don't know, but I must do because I still can't say *red.*

Another laugh falls from his lips, and he starts moving inside me again.

The pain is worse, but there's something sinister about what he's doing that makes me crave more. When he speeds up, every thought flies out of my brain, leaving a void. Then he pulls out of my ass without warning and plunges back into my pussy, rutting into me with a rush of carnal animalistic need that seems to go on forever. Quickly it becomes the cold, hard fucking I've heard my cousin, Raven, talk about.

Everything is beyond what I imagined.

And so is he.

Every inch of me feels like it could shatter, severing me from existence.

It does exactly that when another wild orgasm rips through me. I scream again, throwing my head back at the same time his cock tenses inside my passage. Then warmth heats up my core when he climaxes too.

My God...

I'm burning up. My skin is so hot, I'm going to explode.

I just had wild, crazy sex with a total stranger.

What now, though?

We stay just like this for a few moments until our breaths still.

When I calm down, I feel drained, my body crippled, as if I've been running a week-long marathon.

He pulls out of me and slides off the bed. The sordid thought hits me at that moment that he's done with me now.

What if he tells me to leave?

What if he dismisses me as if what we just did was nothing?

Deciding to avoid the humiliation, I avert my gaze from him and make my way off the bed, but he catches my ankle and yanks me back toward him, flipping me onto my back.

"Where do you think you're going?" His gaze intensifies.

"I thought I had to leave."

"No. You and I aren't finished yet." A lock of his tousled hair falls over his eye, making him look even sexier.

"Aren't we?"

"That was just a taste of what I want to do to you." Kissing the tops of my feet, he makes his way back up to my sore pussy and plants fiery kisses over my mound. "So no, you aren't going anywhere."

When I wake up, it's morning. I'm momentarily disorientated, until I roll onto my side and find myself staring at the god-like man I spent the night with.

He's fast asleep, and I'm lying in his arms.

Memories of last night flood my mind and my body tingles, wanting him again.

We had sex three times, and I'm so sore I can barely move.

I have to move though, because I need to leave.

I can't be here when he wakes.

I have to be gone from this house and his world as if last night never happened. Even though I'll never forget it.

Sliding off the bed, I grab what's left of my dress and inspect it.

It's completely destroyed. I thought I could use the little straps to tie it on me, but that won't work.

Thinking fast, I look around for something else to wear and find the black shirt he was wearing last night lying by the dresser.

I put it on, and it's so big for me it swallows my body. It smells like him too.

This can be something to remember him by.

I look at my handsome stranger and think of how strong and foreboding he looks even in his sleep.

I'm not a virgin anymore. I gave the only thing I had left to this man. Now that I have, I at least get to hold on to that sense of freedom and choice Antonio Marchesi, my soon-to-be bastard husband, won't ever be able to take from me.

I glance around the room and commit what I see to memory. Then I look at my handsome stranger once more and think of what he did for me.

Who is he?

What is he?

I wish I at least knew his name.

Maybe it's better this way, though. It's not like knowing who he is would do me any good. I need to become Persephone Vittorio again, and that means getting on that plane tonight and flying back to New York to the gilded cage that will become my new life.

"My angel," I whisper. That is what he was for me.

The dark, mysterious angel I'll never see again.

2

LUKIYAN

Present Day
L.A., California

In one swift move, I drive my knife into Father Pedro's heart.

His eyes snap wide, then cling to my ruthless gaze as if he can't believe he's actually going to meet his maker.

His last breath comes out in a whoosh, along with the gurgling sound of blood pouring from his heart. As he crosses over to the other side, the light of the living leaves his eyes. Seconds later, his graying head flops back against the leatherback chair, and his body goes limp.

Behind him is a stained glass featuring Jesus and his twelve, but I don't believe any of them will be welcoming Father Pedro through Heaven's gates.

I wouldn't.

The same way I never gave him a chance to beg for his life. I wasn't going to give him an opportunity most don't get.

Just like a shadow, I'd slipped in through the church's narrow hallway leading into his office. Then, without anyone noticing, I killed the guards and came in here to finish the job my Pakhan—the Yurkov's fearsome leader— entrusted to me.

When I twist the knife in Father Pedro's heart, I take pleasure in killing him that much more, issuing exactly what he deserves for his evil extracurricular activities.

I'm a Vor. I was raised in the Bratva, so I know no other way than an eye for an eye and a life for a life. Especially when you're foolish enough to play with the devil.

So, the *good* father here had to pay with his life for using the money we donated to the church to run his human trafficking ring. His specialty was babies and children under ten, but his personal favorite was their organs.

He won't be doing that anymore.

I'm not a good man by any means. And I'm nobody's savior. I was certain I heard the angels scream the moment I stepped on God's doorstep and my unhallowed feet walked through the church.

I probably deserve a torturous death for all I've done, but at least I'm not Father Pedro.

He's one less fucker for the world to worry about now.

The bonus in ending him is that my need to kill has been satisfied tonight.

Killing bastards like him is all I can do to tamp down the rage roiling within

me. Until I dole out my revenge on the motherfucker who killed my sister, killing

is all I can do.

As the dark red blood runs from Father Pedro's deceiving heart, I focus on the color. On how the deep red is so rich and pure, *alive* but not. *Not anymore.*

I haven't been able to look at blood and see it as just *blood* since that fateful night six months ago when I found my sister's body on the floor of her bedroom, surrounded by red rose petals that looked like they were floating in her blood.

Now I see the blood, and while the morbid image of my sister clings to my mind, the memory of the woman I should have long forgotten comes to me too.

My nameless beauty's lips were blood red and shaped like a beating heart.

The memory of our wild night in Brazil still haunts me.

All I have to do is think of her, and I remember warm brown hair sprawled out in long graceful waves against my sheets as I drove into her sweet cunt.

I remember her petite, willowy frame, eroticized by large, fully-rounded breasts and those piercing, amber-colored eyes which spoke of mystery, secrecy, and desperation.

I only went to Brazil to forget.

I needed the break after hunting for Melissa's killer for six months and finding nothing but shit.

My wild encounter with the dark-haired beauty wasn't supposed to happen. Then again, I went to the club that night looking for pussy, and I always get

what I want.

She was different to any other woman I've been with, and I haven't been able to get her out of my head or the taste of her sweet pussy out of my mouth.

Like a masochist, I keep holding on to the memory.

It's a rare day when a soulless creature like me finds a distraction in a woman when he's had so many others.

Maybe it was because I wasn't done with her yet.

Or maybe it was because she was a virgin, and I was the first man to claim every hole in her body and make her mine.

Even to a dark soul like me, there's something meaningful about being the first to claim a woman's virginity.

It's been years since I've fucked a virgin, but never one like her. She hooked me from the moment I saw her on the dance floor and decided she was going to be mine for the night.

When I took her back to the beach house I always rent when I need one of my Brazilian getaways, I knew she must have made some impression on me.

No matter which country I'm in, I never take women home. Yet when I saw her, there was no question about what I was going to do with her.

It pisses me off that I don't know who she is, where she came from, or where she went. I would have looked for her, but I thought I owed her the courtesy of not knowing me.

Certainly, if she could see me now, she would have listened to those instincts of hers that were telling her I'm dangerous.

I could see it in her eyes that she knew she shouldn't be anywhere near a fiend like me, but she still offered herself to me on a decadent platter. And fuck, did she ever taste sweeter than any fruit I've ever had.

Now she's just a memory, and I'm back in L.A.

Back on my mission of death.

Back to being Lukiyan Romanechka, the Obshchak of the Yurkov Bratva. I'm the guy in charge of overseeing the money that comes into the organization and our security —which is why I'm here with Father Pedro.

I inherited the role from my adopted father, Dmitri Kozlov. He and his wife died three years ago in a head-on collision.

My father took care of the enforcers—the assassins— in the Brotherhood, and now I do the same.

I kill for a living.

I pull my knife out of Father Pedro's heart, grab a tissue from the box on the side, and wipe off the blood.

I'm about to place the knife back in its sheath when my phone starts vibrating in my back pocket.

There's only one person who would call me while I'm on the job.

I reach for the phone and see I'm right.

"Hello, Pakhan." I press the phone to my ear. "Mission accomplished."

He knows I would have done my job, but I tell him anyway, to cover myself.

Lucca Dyshekov has always been a friend to me, even before he became the Pakhan a few years back. However, the last thing I want to do is look weak to those I need to show strength. Or seem uninterested in my job when I'm the newest member of the elite group in our Brotherhood

It goes without saying that I haven't been myself since Melissa's death, and everyone knows it. Everyone also knows that the only thing on my mind is finding her killer.

They've been helping me with all the resources at our fingertips, but months ago, the trail ran cold. Knowing so crippled me, placing me in that state of wretched weakness I haven't experienced since I was a child.

"Good job," Lucca says. "I need you to come to the house. We found a lead on Judas Kane."

The moment he says that name, my interest piques, rocketing through the sky.

Judas Kane—my sister's killer.

They finally found a lead on him.

"I'm on my way."

I arrive at Lucca's enormous manor house in record time after riding my motorcycle as if I had the infernal flames of hell on my ass.

I take the sweeping marble stairs leading to his office and find him inside with Aleksei, his second-in-command, and Sovietnik. Both are sitting at the large mahogany desk by the window.

Behind them is an oil painting depicting the Four Horsemen of the Apocalypse. I've always found that painting fitting to who we are and what we do. I feel it now as I approach them.

This is us together—the three members that form the elite. Usually, when we meet here, we talk business. Tonight we'll be plotting death.

"Hey," Lucca greets me as I take my seat opposite Aleksei.

"Hi, what did you find?"

"Something solid, but it's not going to be easy." Lucca straightens with a tense look on his face, tucking a lock of his shoulder-length hair behind his ear.

Aleksei clenches his jaw, and I know from the strained look in his eyes that although we have a lead, whatever they have to tell me isn't going to be something I want to hear.

It's probably more shit about Melissa to taint her image.

"Judas is working with the Camorra Syndicate," Lucca says.

Camorra Syndicate? No wonder we couldn't find him. I suspected links to some big organization. I was right.

The Camorra Syndicate is run by Tobias Rivera. He has branches here in the States and Europe the same way we do but he's based in Italy. Unlike the Bratva, they're a smaller entity with massive power and the right connections to keep them that way.

"Where is he?" I ball my fist.

"We don't know that part yet," Lucca answers. "However, I'm hoping what we've found will help us locate him."

"I managed to intercept a remote call while tracking a black-market dealer in Uzbekistan. I suspected the guy was linked to Judas because of the items he was selling," Aleksei explains. Judas Kane is an assassin who's been linked to some of the world's deadliest criminals and organizations. He's also a black-market dealer, so anything black-market related would be right up his alley. "It turns out this guy and Judas both work with Emilio Vittorio."

I've heard of him. Emilio is Tobias Rivera's cousin and the second seat clan member on the Camorra Syndicate's council.

He currently lives in New York and makes his fortune from his casinos and property across the globe. There isn't a country on this earth that doesn't have some sort of business owned by that man.

The motherfucker also dabbles in the sex trade.

Cautiousness invades Lucca's expression when I look back at him.

"When we looked into things further, we realized Melissa met Judas through Emilio," Lucca explains. "She worked for him at the L.A. branch of his escort service called Escape."

My blood heats with the rage I'm trying to control. I didn't know Emilio owned Escape.

Things are starting to make sense now.

After Melissa died I found out she was on hardcore drugs and worked as an escort. I just didn't know it was this bad.

The girls who work at Escape get a fuck load of money to be whatever they are paid to be because they cater for men with dark, twisted tastes.

The girls are the desperate kind who will sell their souls if they need to. It grieves me that my sister became that way and never thought she could come to me for help.

While I thought she was doing well in school and preparing for college, she was doing shit like this to deal with the grief she felt over losing our parents.

Lucca slides a sheet of paper over to me.

It's a V.I.P client list, with a listing of the girls they were each allocated. Circled in the center is the fake name Melissa used—*Jennifer Carlton*. Next to her name is her client's - Judas Kane.

As everything falls into place in my mind, I clench my jaw and narrow my eyes. My heart gallops frantically in my chest when I think of how that bastard must have degraded my sweet sister.

I know she was to blame for her actions, but when Emilio hired her, she would have been a minor in a vulnerable state who couldn't help herself.

She was barely eighteen when she died.

That makes Emilio just as guilty as Judas for her death.

"Emilio is arranging a job with Judas," Lucca continues. "We don't know the details of that job or when they'll be meeting, only that he'll be in New York at some point in the next few weeks."

"So I'll go to New York and find him," I cut in.

Lucca eyes me firmly, hardening his stare "You know as well as I do that if it were as simple as that, we'd already be there. The moment you breathe a word to anyone about him, that's it. Your chance of finding him will disappear. He already knows you're looking for him. He practically invited you to look."

"I know."

The whole thing has been a game to that motherfucker.

The roses scattered around Melissa's body, along with the knife wounds in her head, heart, and stomach, were the only clues of what happened to her.

And also, who did it.

That's his style, like some freaking calling card.

He wanted those she left behind to know it was he who killed her. And know that even with all the strength of the men in the Bratva and our allies combined, it would take a miracle to find him.

Judas Kane is notorious among the world's most dangerous because he can become a ghost when he needs to be. He can choose when to exist and when to fade away.

That doesn't matter to me because I'm going to find him no matter how long it takes, and he'll die at my hands the same way he killed my sister.

"I have an idea," Lucca says. "One that might be tricky but worth a shot."

"What is it?" *I'll do anything.*

"Emilio has a job opening for a new guard on his personal security team. You could do it." He raises his brows. "Go in and get close to him."

I keep my gaze trained on him, seeing where he's taking this idea. It wouldn't be the first time I've gone undercover. This is just the first time it would truly matter.

"Get close and find out when he'll be meeting Judas," I fill in, and he nods.

"No one can trace your links to us, or our allies. That will be your advantage."

It will.

Although Melissa took our adopted parents family name, I kept Romanechka to remember my birth mother. Everyone respected that because at twelve-years-old, I was an older child when the Kozlovs' adopted me. It would have been weird for me to suddenly change my name, especially when I didn't want to. It was fine for Melissa because she was only five-years-old.

Years later, as I took on my duties in the Bratva, being Lukiyan *Romanechka* worked to my advantage as there has never been anything to link me to the organization.

Try to look me up, and all you'll find are the details of a man with a troubled past and a history of violence. Nothing about the mafia, though.

People call me the Shadow because I can blend in and be whoever I want to be.

"Take your guards," Lucca continues. "Aleksei will also go with you as backup, and we can set things up from here to move in when you need us."

"Thank you."

"No need to thank me. Vengeance was always going to be ours. Your father was good to me right from when I was a boy. He trained me, like many others, and was like a father to me."

That's my father all over—the man who adopted two orphans siblings because he wanted to keep us together.

He was as ruthless as he needed to be, but he had the right amount of heart that allowed him to stay in touch with humanity.

Aleksei moves the file in front of him over to me. "This is what I have so far on Emilio."

I open the file and take note of the picture of Emilio on the front page.

With his tousled salt-and-pepper hair and ghostly pale skin, he looks like a cross between a pirate lord and a vampire. He's in his mid-fifties but looks older because of the scars marring the left side of his face, and one blinding his right eye, which is just a ball of grayish white. It makes him look like the embodiment of evil itself.

I flip the page and my hand instantly stills, frozen in shock, when my gaze lands on the image of the beautiful brown-haired woman with amber eyes I spent the night with in Brazil.

For a moment, my mind slips, and I wonder if I've fallen into some kind of twisted dream where I've conjured her from my thoughts.

I'm tempted to believe I'm seeing things, but I know I'm not.

It's her.

"Who is she to him?" I rest a thumb on the side of her face, remembering the silky feel of her smooth, creamy skin.

"His daughter, Persephone."

Daughter?

What a coincidence of shit.

And *Persephone?*

That's her actual name? Like the mythical goddess.

I guess that would make me her Hades because I'm staring down at her picture, finally knowing who she is, and I still feel like I'm not done with her yet.

"I didn't know he had a daughter." I tap the picture then quickly make a fist.

"Only a few people outside family and friends know," Aleksei explains. "I gathered information of all the people you need to be aware of. Obviously, she's the most important."

What was she doing in Brazil?

Never mind that. The real question is, could she compromise this mission for me?

No...

I almost smile.

She didn't want me to know who she was because she's Emilio Vittorio's daughter.

Emilio Vittorio's virgin daughter shouldn't have been all alone in a club, much less anywhere near me.

I can guarantee that I shouldn't have been the first man to make her virgin cunt bleed.

That means she's not going to say anything if or when she sees me again.

"She's getting married to Antonio Marchesi in a month's time, and then she'll be going to Italy," Aleksei explains further. "I think this meeting with Judas will likely take place before her wedding."

Wedding. Wow. My breath lodges in my throat as if someone built a dam around my lungs.

Maybe that was what she was running from.

What the fuck kind of situation have I truly landed myself in?

No matter what it is, this has to work.

This is that miracle I needed to find Judas.

"When can I leave?"

"Tonight," Lucca replies.

I dip my head reverently. "I'll pack my things."

One last look at the image of the girl who offered her virginity to me, and I

close the file. Her face still lingers in my mind though. The same way it has for the last three months.

I'll never forget how ruthlessly I owned her body, nor how much I craved

more.

And still do.

Sweet, angelic Persephone, I still want you.

That, however, is not going to stop me from killing your father.

3

PERSEPHONE

New York

The truth is what you make of it.

So is reality.

In my reality, I'm little more than the nightingale trapped in a cage.

Behind my bars, I try to survive by thinking of the only thing I can that will keep me alive—*freedom.*

Sitting in this living room for the last half an hour, where the ghosts of my mother and sister still haunt, has felt like being trapped in the lion's den. I have my bastard husband-to-be sitting beside me, and my cousin in the armchair opposite us holding our wedding registration documents.

That glimmer of freedom keeps my heart beating and strengthens the threads I'm barely hanging on to.

The focus is just strong enough to keep me going until I escape—if I can pull it off. I always have to bear that part in mind because my plans could go to hell and get people I love killed.

It's bad enough I'm still stuck in this game of pretense where I look like I'm going through with the marriage, but I would die if I lost another loved one.

The wedding is in three weeks, but I'll be long gone before that time if all goes to plan.

I always knew I'd have an arranged marriage. I just didn't know when it would happen or to whom it was going to be.

What a fool I was to believe that trip to Brazil could have been anything other than what it turned out to be when my life has never been mine.

The trip was just another façade of shit concocted by my father to control me.

Going there was a matter of convenience because Antonio and his family were going to be there too.

Father knows how much I hate Antonio, so I can't help but feel he did this to punish me—*punish me for living.*

That's what pushed me into the arms of a stranger. I never wanted my first time to be with the devil beside me.

Thank God for Uncle Frankie. He's like my mediator. That night, he understood my need to bolt and covered for me.

He's the only reason I was able to enjoy my escape with my handsome stranger.

Releasing a slow, silent sigh, I mentally count backwards from thirty the way my therapist taught me and try to keep my focus on the end goal.

Raven places the documents with the images of the wedding venue designs
on the coffee table.

As she spreads out each one so we can see the beautiful gold and burgundy designs, I try not to grab them and throw them through the long French windows across from us.

She's fully aware of my hatred for the man next to me, so she probably expects me to snap.

I'm amazed at her calm, professional manner. She's even dressed in a business suit today. Raven is two years older than me and more flamboyant.

She tones it down though, whenever she's around my father or any of the men in the alliance.

Setting her shoulders back, she plasters a smile on her face as she returns her focus to Antonio and me. "This is what the hall will look like. I went with what you requested." She speaks directly to Antonio since I didn't make any requests.

He nods, giving her that smug expression I loathe when he catches the slight tremor in her hands.

She's as afraid of him as I am.

I fucking hate admitting fear, but it's true.

Strength sometimes means accepting weaknesses. I

know how to choose my battles and when to retreat until I can do better—which is what I'm doing now as I'm forced to sit through this meeting.

We're supposed to meet the new bodyguard in a little while, but Antonio insisted on a quick *catch-up*.

"This is all fine," Antonio replies, steepling his fingers. "What about the catering?"

As Raven starts giving him the rundown of what she's arranged with the caterers, I allow my mind to drift to the only good thing that happened in Brazil—the night I lost myself in *Mr. Gorgeous.*

His handsome face still lingers in my mind, and his touch still ravages my body.

I'm sure he's long forgotten me, but I'll never forget him, nor all the ways he claimed me.

I'm not sure who would be able to forget a man like him. Just thinking of him stirs the desperate need which ravaged my body that night.

Sometimes, during the moments I allow Mr. Gorgeous to invade my mind, I fear people will know what I'm thinking. Sure, I know it's ridiculous to worry over such a thing. But I do.

As much as I trust Raven, I never told her about him. She also doesn't know of my plans to escape.

Although I know she'd support me, keeping both secrets from her is safer.

Any other woman my age in the clan alliance wouldn't have been able to do what I did and get away with it. Under contract from birth, we're supposed to remain virgins until the day we get married, or at the very least until The Exchange.

Like everything else to do with our clan in the Camorra, The Exchange is another archaic Machiavellian activity of control where fathers sign over their daughters to their future husbands.

My Exchange, when I was handed over to Antonio, was what happened to me in Brazil. I unknowingly walked into a trap.

Once contracts were signed, everything that belonged to me, from my body to my staff, became Antonio's.

Obviously, there'll be hell to pay when Antonio finds out I'm not a virgin, but the risk I took that night was worth it.

The loss of my virginity is nothing compared to what he'll gain from marrying me and being next in line to take over my father's empire. He'll also gain his seat on the Camorra Syndicate when my father retires.

"Everything else is taken care of," Raven says with a firm nod. "And all the guests have RSVPd."

"Great." Antonio gives me a hard stare, probably because I haven't said shit since we walked in here.

Why should I talk when I don't care for any of this?

"Anything you want to add, Persephone?" His voice has an arctic edge that chills me from the inside out.

"No." I'll say no more than that. Anything else will get me in trouble.

This is the second time I've seen him since Brazil, and I

haven't forgotten his threats to make good on his word to fuck me.

I've experienced his brutality enough to know he was serious and would force himself on me.

Both times he's been alone with me saw him shoving his cock down my throat to teach me a lesson.

The first time happened in Brazil. The next was here in this very room.

He stares me down as if he can read my mind and see my trepidation.

I know I'm a joke to him.

What else can I be?

Right now, I'm helpless. I'm supposed to be Persephone Vittorio, the daughter of one of the most powerful men on earth, but I can't do anything more than what I'm doing to save myself.

Antonio knows this is driving me crazy and is delighting in it because he hates that I don't worship him the way other women do for his money and his looks.

"I just need the two of you to sign off on these documents and the registration details for the church," Raven says. "Once you do that, I'll fax them back to the planning team."

"Perfect." Antonio takes the pen from Raven.

She cuts me a glance when he leans forward to sign the documents, and I give her a weary smile of appreciation.

She's going to be my maid of honor. Right now, she's my pillar of strength.

When we returned to New York, she offered to organize the wedding.

Not because she was happy about my upcoming nuptials, but because she knew how much this whole ordeal sucked the life out of me.

I had what I thought was going to be a promising career dancing with the New York City Ballet, but that's now a dream I have to forget.

I've been dancing from the time I learned to walk, so Raven knows how much my soul shattered when I was told I wouldn't be able to finish my studies and training at Juilliard. That also wiped out all my hopes to dance with the New York City Ballet.

Antonio finishes signing the documents and hands the pen to me.

I sign and pray none of this comes to be.

"Raven, please excuse us. I need to speak to Persephone alone." Although he's talking to her, he keeps his eyes nailed to me.

"Sure." Raven gazes at me with sorrowful eyes.

I know she's sorry. I'm sorry, too.

As soon as she walks through the door, he stands, and suddenly, the walls around me feel like they're shrinking away.

I glare up at him, and when he steps forward, I get up, not wanting to give him the chance to hit me like last time.

He laughs at my obvious fear and tilts his head to the side, allowing his dark locks to fall over his face.

"What do you want?" I steel my spine, trying to summon courage. The worst thing I could do is show him just how much he gets under my skin.

"You."

"I thought you already had me."

He inches closer. "You know what I mean. Once I have that cherry between your legs, I'll have all of you."

Bastard.

I'd love to tell him the cherry between my legs no longer exists, and I gave it away, just so he couldn't have it.

Antonio thinks I'm the good little girl waiting to do as she's told. Good girls like me are raised from birth to do just that. We're taught to respect and obey. *Always.*

So he'd never guess that I broke the rules, and I plan to do so much worse.

He touches my cheek and runs a finger down to the hollow of my neck. "I've discussed the idea of you moving in with me sooner with your father." His smile becomes menacing. "Things will be easier if you're with me."

Easier to get me in his bed, he means. He's such an asshole. I'm just lucky he hasn't raped me yet.

Things have been set up so we'll be living in his home in New York for three weeks after the wedding before flying out to Italy. I'm supposed to move in the week before. But I won't be doing any of it.

Not the wedding, the fucking moving in, nor the sham marriage.

The fundraiser in five days' time will be my ticket out.

I want to tell him to go fuck himself and yank his

stupid engagement ring off my finger and throw it in his face. But I hold back.

I just need to be patient and keep my head above water for the next few days.

Five days. That's all it is now.

I can do that.

I've managed the last three months. This is just the final hurdle to jump over.

When he steps closer, I move back. Another step, and I repeat.

We do this uncoordinated tango until back hits the wall, and he's giving me a shit-eating grin. Dark eyes roam over my body, and my stomach tightens into hard knots.

I can have a strong mind that will allow me to escape reality, but I'm no match for him in physical strength.

So when he cups my breast and squeezes, I know if I fight him off, things will be worse for me.

"I simply can't wait to fuck you." He brushes his nose over mine and tries to kiss me, but I turn my face away, barely managing to avoid his lips.

We've never kissed, and I want to keep it that way. I don't want him to touch any part of me, but a kiss feels far too intimate—almost more than sex.

That's why I don't ever want to remember his lips on mine.

"Still fighting me?"

"You know I don't want you." I'm always upfront, so there's no room for confusion. I want him to always know that I will never give in.

"Yet, I want you so badly." He chuckles deep and low, lifting the hem of my skirt so he can cup my sex.

"My father will be here soon."

He answers by squeezing my breasts harder. "Your body belongs to me now. I'm sure he'll understand if I want to feel you up."

How gross.

"You think it's appropriate for my father to see you feeling me up?"

"It doesn't matter who sees me. I've always wanted you."

"Is that what you tell your whores when you're fucking them? That you've always wanted me?" I know he sleeps around, and that's fine by me.

Better for him to get it somewhere else than from me.

"You know you're the only whore I want."

"I'm not a whore."

"You suck dick like a whore."

"Fuck you." I try to pull away, but he shoves me into the wall so hard I knock the back of my head.

"You fucking bastard." *Fuck it.* I've had enough. I hate it when he hurts me.

"You have a death wish, don't you?" He steps forward.

"No, I don't."

"I think you do." His lips quirk into a sadistic smile, and my skin crawls. "I don't think you truly know who I am."

"I know who you are, Antonio."

"Then you don't know *what* I am."

Oh, I beg to differ. I'm fully aware of what kind of creature this motherfucker is.

At twenty-eight years old, he's the eldest of Mario Marchesi's two sons. Mario and my father have been friends since birth, which means I've always known his asshole sons. I never wanted to be at the mercy of either of them.

Now I'm owned by the worst one. Lawrence, Antonio's older brother, is considered the less psychotic of the two.

Seeing the uncanny look enter Antonio's eyes reminds me of the first time I saw him kill.

I was twelve years old. He killed one of his guards because the man was late for work. The guard apologized. He had to take his baby to the doctor because she was sick. Antonio made him believe it was okay—like he had hope. But as soon as the man turned his back, Antonio shot him in the head with a smile on his face.

Seven years on, and that smile is still there.

"I'm aware of what you are, Antonio. You're the kind of man who takes pleasure in unhappiness. You're happy when I'm sad. You love when I cry, and you love that I can't do the one thing I love. Ballet was my life, and you made me give it up, just because you could."

"*I* am your life, now." He quickly shows me there's nothing human in him when he grabs my throat and squeezes hard. "You are mine, and it's time you started acting like it. Do you hear me?"

"Yes," I choke out, trying to catch my breath.

"Push me again, and I'll break your legs. Then you can truly kiss dancing goodbye."

My God.

My heart is already weeping for the loss of my dream, but to break my legs?

What a bastard. I can't imagine taking pleasure in another person's pain the way he does. Yet he would break me beyond repair.

And my father would allow him to batter me because he doesn't care.

There's nothing *anyone* can do to help me or stop Antonio from hurting me because that's the law of our alliance. I belong to him, and he can do whatever he wants to me.

"Do you understand me?" he prods.

"Yes."

I understand perfectly, and no fucking way am I going to allow him to break my legs so I can't run away.

When I came back to the world of the living, I promised myself I would achieve all my dreams, but more than anything, I promised myself I'd live. I'd live for those who sacrificed themselves for me to have a life, and I'd live for me.

So I'll do what I must, even if that means playing devil's advocate.

"Good girl. If we had time, I'd throw you down and fuck your brains out." He squeezes my throat tighter, and I gasp for air. I try to pull out of his grasp, but he tightens his grip. "But soon, Persephone. *Soon.*"

A knock on the door saves me. That should be my father and the new bodyguard.

Antonio releases me, and I cough when the air rushes back into my lungs.

I try to gather myself as the door swings open and Father and Uncle Frankie walk in, but the man who comes in next has me wondering if my eyes are screwing with me.

My brain skitters to an abrupt stop, and every cell in my body freezes as Mr. Gorgeous from Brazil walks in as if he's materializing from my thoughts. The only difference being, in my head, he was shirtless or completely naked. Now he's wearing a suit without a tie, looking like he just stepped out of a photoshoot for some classy men's fashion magazine.

My throat clogs from the scathing shock racing through my veins, and my heart stops beating as if someone just switched it off.

Is it really him?

Those eyes. Those blue, blue, blue eyes bore into me, and that sinful smile tips his full, sensual lips.

That neck tattoo and the other artful designs that line his ears and the sides of his head are unmistakable, along with the numbered tattoos on his fingers.

It's him.

It's really him.

Clearly the Universe has pulled some kind of joke on me.

He's here in my world, in my life, in my nightmare.

And he's as real as I am.

"This is Antonio Marchesi, my soon-to-be son-in-law, and Persephone, my daughter," Father says, pulling me from my shock.

Mr. Gorgeous steps forward and holds out his hand to shake mine.

I lift one trembling hand and give it to him the same way I did in the club when he asked me to go home with him.

The moment my skin makes contact with his large hand, that familiar zap of electricity sparks in my soul just like it did that night when I wanted him, and nothing else mattered.

As if he can tell what I'm thinking, his gaze flicks down to my hand in his, but it's only for a moment.

"Hello, Persephone. I'm Lukiyan Romanechka."

Lukiyan Romanechka.

That's his name.

Now I know it.

4

LUKIYAN

Look at the way she's staring back at me.

That's not just shock on Persephone Vittorio's pretty face.

It's arousal.

Yes, her sun-kissed skin has gone pale, but the slight hint of pink flushed over her cheeks and the fire flickering in her eyes reminisce of that night we devoured each other.

I wonder if she realizes she's looking at me like she wants to fuck me again.

Just like that fated night when we met, her hand feels small in mine, and she looks tiny. Tiny like a little fairy. An erotic version of Tinkerbell with her round tits and shapely hips.

Fuck me. Not even five minutes into the job, and I've already lost the game.

And my shit. Like I knew it would, it's grating on my nerves that she doesn't belong to me.

I've spent the last few days prepping myself for this moment. I told myself I had to focus and couldn't allow anything or anyone to get in the way of what I want.

Now that I'm standing in front of her, all I can think of is what it would feel like to be inside her again.

As the seconds tick by, I conjure the image of us angry fucking, where I'd slam her against the wall and fuck her so hard, she'd pass out.

Emilio clears his throat in an exaggerated manner, snapping us both from our daze. Instantly, Persephone pulls her hand from mine and forces a smile.

The black patch Emilio is wearing over his bad eye seems to overpower his face, but I can see the thin line of displeasure on his lips, showing he's not fond of his daughter's obvious interest in me.

And neither is her husband-to-be.

Raw jealousy invades Antonio's eyes when I look at him and see I've already made an enemy of him.

"Nice to meet you," Persephone says, cutting her father a cautious glance as if she's checking for his approval.

I know from that brief exchange that he's the dictator, and she's the perpetual child.

"Likewise." I keep my tone measured to mask my emotions.

"Lukiyan is the new bodyguard I was telling you guys about," Frankie explains.

I did my interview with him first before meeting

Emilio. The two look similar even though Emilio is older by ten years. Their personalities are where they differ. Frankie has a lighter temperament. His smiles come easy, while I can't imagine Emilio smiling at all.

"Lukiyan will be moving into the guest house," Emilio states, and Persephone stares back at him wide-eyed as if he just slapped her.

I'll admit I was surprised to hear this was a live-in position, but it works greatly to my benefit for getting close.

This way, I'm exactly where I need to be for as long as I want.

"The guest house?" Her voice comes out in a stutter, and her skin actually goes paler than it was before.

"Yes. I trust there will be no problems."

"No. Not at all. There won't be any problems."

Liar. We both know I'm the problem. A very big one, but she's a problem for me too.

"Don't worry, I have my eye on her," Antonio says, giving me an insincere smile as he slips a possessive arm around Persephone's tiny waist.

I could almost laugh. The motherfucker is trying to show me who she belongs to. *Prick.* I'd love to set him straight and inform him that I had his woman first.

"I'm sure you do." I dip my head, playing the game as issue my own phony-as-hell smile.

When he plants a kiss on her forehead, I don't miss the way Persephone goes rigid against him.

She looks trapped, which tells me what I need to know

about their relationship too. Or at least what I want to see, which is that she doesn't want him.

She doesn't look at him the way she looks at me.

I've been in L.A. for the last three days, checking things out with Aleksei.

I did my research on this idiot too, as thoroughly as I looked into everyone else I'll be interacting with while I'm here. Antonio Marchesi is a year older than me and we pretty much have the same background when it comes to education and interests. His family is nearly as wealthy as the Vittorios, but they don't have the same power.

While I know never to underestimate anyone, to me he's seems just like every other entitled fucker in their circle who thinks they own the world.

"Alright, you've met everyone now," Emilio says before the awkward silence and tension can fill the space between us. "We have a busy schedule, so we'll catch up with you all later."

"I guess I'll see you later, then," I tell Persephone.

Her amber-colored eyes become more rounded as she catches the hidden promise in my words.

We need to talk.

She'll know that.

There's no way either of us can pretend Brazil never happened. More importantly, I need to make sure she doesn't pose a threat to me and compromise my goals.

Now that I've seen her and witnessed the interaction between her father and fiancé, I feel more confident that she won't be. But I need to be sure.

Failure is not an option. This mission is too important for me to go on assumptions. I don't want to risk fucking this up in any way, shape, or form.

"Later, yes." She nods with a slight clench in her jaw.

Although her eyes cling to me, I don't look back when Emilio motions toward the door.

We leave Frankie with Persephone and Antonio and proceed down the corridor. I can still feel her gaze on me when I'm out of the room, but I break the connection from my awareness so I can focus.

"Let's go to my office first so we can finish the paperwork and talk some more about the job," Emilio suggests, glancing at me out of the corner of his good eye.

"Sure."

We continue down a winding hall that looks as classy as the rest of the mansion. It has black marble floors, creamy satin-wallpapered walls and chandeliers hanging from the ornate ceiling, which shows Renaissance paintings akin to the Sistine Chapel in Rome.

The entire house reeks of power, not just the power that comes from being wealthy, but the type of power that stamps ownership on a person. *Or people.*

In the Bratva, we have ownership like that. But unless you are the Pakhan with your name attached to the empire, you're owned by him too.

Emilio takes me to his office, which is on the same floor but on the other side of the house.

His office, full of antique-looking wooden furniture and a shelf with leather-bound books, is exactly what I would expect for someone of his caliber. The scent of leather and power fills the room, along with that ominous presence of the unknown.

Emilio's wary of me. I can sense it.

He can't figure me out, and he's trying to. I know the bastard is even questioning his decision to hire me, although I got the job hands down because I was the best suited.

What I had were the right kind of references to make me look good on paper, and to him.

In the Bratva, we have all the right connections to make anything look the way we want. So when I handed Emilio references from Miguel Hernandez, head of the Diaz Cartel in Colombia, and Cillian Montgomery, head of the Irish mafia in New York, I knew I had the job. Emilio has worked with both men many times over the last two decades. They're also the kind of men of power those from the Camorra are drawn to.

What he doesn't know is that they have a secret alliance with my Pakhan.

Emilio Vittorio is no fool. I'm sure he at least suspects something, but he's a man of facts. He wouldn't cut off his nose when he's already lost an eye. Especially when there's no evidence of duplicity or malevolence.

I could be wrong about the distrust I'm sensing. Perhaps it's not that at all and what he can smell is my thirst for vengeance.

Maybe he can sense that I want to slice his throat and

cut out his heart so he can watch me chop it into pieces and serve it to his dogs for dinner.

All in good time. All… in good time.

"Take a seat." He nods to the chair in front of his desk, and I sit.

He sits too, in his winged leather chair and reaches for the humidor on his left.

He opens it, holding it out to me so I can take one of his Cubans.

I do to be polite.

He takes one for himself and lights both our cigars, all while keeping his good eye trained on me.

"May I call you Lukiyan?"

"Of course, *Boss.*"

"Great. Lukiyan. My daughter is beautiful, isn't she?" The question throws me and I'm not sure how to answer other than with the obvious.

"Yes, she is."

He searches my eyes, still trying to figure me out. My professional poker face, however, is one that offers iron-clad control over my emotions so I can keep people out. The only person who could see through the windows of my soul is dead. I couldn't keep anything from my sister, even though she succeeded in keeping so much from me.

Taking a drag on his cigar, he slowly releases the smoke. "She takes after her mother in appearance."

He points to an oil painting on the wall opposite us of a beautiful young woman who indeed looks like Persephone. The only exception is her platinum-blonde hair.

I'm amazed Emilio has a painting of his dead wife when he's been remarried for the last three years. There doesn't appear to be any pictures of his new wife in here, nor of his daughters. I'd learned Persephone had a twin who died two years ago.

While his wife was murdered on these very grounds along with his older brother in what could only be described as a massacre, there was no cause of death listed for Persephone's twin, Athena.

I think either she killed herself or something more sinister occurred that Emilio doesn't want people to know about.

Every family has secrets. I'm sure this one is no different.

"The resemblance is striking," I observe.

"Indeed. But she's like me in every other way." His lips move into a ghost of a smile, then return to a hard line. "Nevertheless, she's also young and impressionable and unavailable. Understand?"

Loud and clear. Daddy Dearest is handing me the warning to stay away from his daughter. It's a warning I would follow with ease if I didn't know what his princess tastes like.

"I do."

"Does that mean I can trust you to keep your dick in your pants?" His expression grows serious, and there's a murderous look in his eyes.

"Yes, you can." I say the words even though he looks like he doesn't believe me.

"Good. I'm glad we have that understanding. You come highly recommended by men I know who don't stand for shit. I don't stand for shit either. You're going to be living in my home and I don't want any trouble." He straightens. "Persephone is promised to Antonio. They will be married in three weeks and moving to Italy. While she's still in my care, I need to know you'll take care of her if anything happens."

"Of course." I narrow my gaze and puff on my cigar. If I'm not mistaken, he sounds like he's expecting something to happen. "Is there something I should be aware of?"

I feel like a hypocrite asking that question when I'm the wolf in sheep's clothing out for blood.

"All I need you to do is keep your eyes open. Your time will be split between this house and the hotels. Watch the place and eliminate any threats. But if something happens, especially to me, I want you to get my daughter to safety. Can I trust you to do that, Mr. Romanechka?"

I'm amazed. At first sight, he seems to be a man who doesn't care much about anything, but he wears his love for his daughter like a heart on a sleeve.

"You can." As I say the words, I feel like I'm not just assuring him.

I'm saying them for myself, too, because she feels like mine to protect.

5

LUKIYAN

"So, how did it go?" Aleksei asks.

"It's been a long fucking day of playing the new guy."

Pressing the phone to my ear, I open the door to the quaint little cottage at the edge of the lake I'll be staying in until I leave here—*whenever that will be.*

Today I went from one end of New York to the other as I travelled back and forth to the different sites I'd be working at. The most important thing I did was bug the systems so we can monitor everything that's happening.

Aleksei and the team are staying at the house in Long Island my father used as a base when he had business here. They'll be monitoring all of Emilio's emails and conversations while I'll be right in the action, ready to rain down Armageddon when Judas shows up.

"I need a joint." I sigh deeply.

"I'm sure you have one of those." He chuckles.

"I do." I walk into the living room and set my bag next

to the rest of my stuff on the floor. I moved my things in this morning before I met everyone and got the tour of the house.

"We've been monitoring, but there's nothing to report yet, but of course, it's early days."

I'm glad Lucca allowed Aleksei to come with me.

Apart from the fact that he can find information on anybody, he's the closest thing I have to a best friend. He's a man I know I can trust with the secrets I choose to share, and my life. We'd probably be closer if I didn't always try to keep people at a distance all the time, but I got that from my sordid childhood.

"Nothing on my end either." *Nothing relevant.*

"I don't believe that." His voice holds an air of disbelief and mischief. I know he's referring to Persephone, but I'm not divulging.

Only tell people what they need to know.

That's what my birth mother used to say. Although the memories of her face have faded, her words are still engraved on my heart. So, I tend to withhold anything close to me that's not relevant to work.

That's why I didn't tell Aleksei about my encounter with Persephone in Brazil. Nevertheless, I know he suspects I'm fascinated with her.

When you work with someone day in and day out, they can pick up on things like that.

"You're seriously not going to tell me about the girl?" He prods.

"There's nothing to say."

"You didn't even talk to her?"

"Aleksei, drop it." I really don't want to talk about Persephone Vittorio now, or any other time. I'm having a hard time as it is keeping my thoughts and my dick under control.

"Ostanovka, mudak," he curses in Russian, calling me an asshole. He calls me that more times than he uses my name. "Come on, I'm just going for something light before we get down to business. You have to at least tell me if she's as pretty in real life as she is in her pictures."

I roll my eyes, even though he can't see me. "Yes." That's something I could have told him before we even stepped on the plane to head here.

"At least I got that out of you."

"You fucker." I smirk.

"Whatever, I'll check in tomorrow."

"Cool."

"Over and out."

"Do svidaniya."

He hangs up and I slump against the wall.

It's nearly ten. My normal working day might end much later than this.

Depending on the week, I'm supposed to work three to four long days.

Today doesn't count because it was my induction. On my days off, I'm welcome to stay on the grounds of the manor, but I'm going to use that time to check in with Aleksei and the team.

The sooner I can get things done here and find Judas,

the quicker I can get back to L.A. and pick up the broken pieces of a life without my sister.

At least, being by myself in this cottage allows me some privacy to think and drop my mask. As the grounds of the manor are extensive and I'm on the other side, I'm completely outside of everyone's orbit. Richard and Gio, the other two live-in guards are near the woods where there are more people.

The only thing left to do today is speak to Princess Persephone.

She should be home in the next ten minutes.

Apparently, she went shopping for the wedding with her cousin.

I grab my laptop and sit on the sofa nearest the door.

I want to see who's inside the house before I make my move.

When I tap into the surveillance, I find Emilio and his wife, Alecia, in their bedroom. Both are sitting in bed reading the newspaper.

Good. Neither looks like they'll be leaving the room for the rest of the night.

I quickly look over the grounds, finding the other guards at their posts. When I switch back to the main house, I'm just in time to see the princess walking up the wide marble stairs.

I keep my eyes riveted to her and her slender body as she proceeds to her room, which is actually more like a little apartment with its own living room area and kitchenette.

As she walks into her actual bedroom, the screen goes blank, and I'm prompted to put in a password.

Emilio is a clever man; he's not going to want his guards spying on his beautiful daughter.

He'll also know who put the password in so he can be sure they were watching his daughter's private quarters for the right reasons.

I might have inherited my place in the Bratva from my father, but I earned my stripes because I'm a tech genius. So I don't need to put a password in.

I simply bypass it and pick up on my viewing of the beauty.

Persephone walks over to the queen-size bed in the center, covered in silky sky-blue sheets which match the curtains.

She sits with her shoulders slumped, worry evident on her face.

Is she worried about me?

She must know I wouldn't have said anything about our wild encounter in Brazil, but like me, she'll want to be sure. I'm sure I could cause all sorts of problems by spilling the truth, but that would ruin everything for me.

I'd learned that her mother is Brazilian with family who still live in Sao Paulo.

I figured that's why Persephone was there, and since I was told she got engaged three months ago, I can only assume we happened that night because of that.

I don't know, though. That could just be me wanting to believe what I want because I still want her.

She pushes to her feet, loosens her hair so it flows down her shoulders, and starts taking off her clothes.

Blood rushes straight to my dick when she unveils her naked body. She looks like a pure vision of sex and temptation. Just like the mythical goddess she is.

I love that she doesn't seem to know the effect of her beauty. She didn't on that night we first met.

That night, innocence collided with darkness.

Two things that should never meet.

It's doing it again now as I look over her perfection and the imperfection she tries to cover with her tattoo.

There's a scar beneath it. I can't quite see it now, but I saw it the night we spent together. Of course, I wondered how she got it, but like now, I'm more interested in the rest of her perfect body.

Her breasts are swollen with arousal, the points of her light pink nipples tight and taut.

The light glistens on her golden skin, inviting me to fixate on her clean- shaven pussy, and I can't believe it's been three months since I last touched her.

Or that I haven't been with a woman since.

The usual women threw themselves at me, but I just couldn't see past the angelic face of the woman I claimed in Brazil.

Now I know her name, and she's on the screen right before me.

I told myself my hiatus was down to focusing on finding Judas. However, deep down, I knew that wasn't true.

Persephone walks over to the nightstand, opens the drawer, and takes out a velvet pouch.

When she pulls out a vibrator, my dick goes from semi-mast to erect within seconds.

She crawls onto the bed, giving me a good view of her ass, and as she rests back against the stack of pillows, spreading her legs wide, I get an even better view of her pussy.

Placing her fingers into her pussy, she holds the vibrator to her clit and starts pleasuring herself.

Fucking hell. I've never seen anything sexier or hot as fuck.

My eyes are superglued to the screen, not daring to look away. Not for a second.

As I watch her, I know she's not thinking about Antonio. I just know there's no way such pleasure could be on her face if she were.

So is she thinking of me?

The torture of seeing the pleasure on her face as she works the vibrator over her clit and squeezes her breasts sends my hand straight into my pants so I can palm my dick. There's already pre-cum on the tip, and my balls have drawn up like they're about to explode.

As she strokes herself, I fist my length, pumping hard along the shaft as pleasure courses through me hard and wild.

I imagine her mouth on my dick, taking me in and sucking me with her little tongue stroking my skin. Then I recall with perfect clarity that it actually happened.

I had her.

I remember those innocent eyes beaming up at me as she kneeled before me and I fucked her face.

The only thing that was missing from that fantasy was hearing her scream my name.

The pleasure on her face is intoxicating and maddening, so potent it's bringing a man like me to the brink of his peak.

I unleash, pumping so hard I roar when I come.

Fuck.

As it pours out of me, I continue watching her, listening to her moan. She hasn't come yet, but that's because I'm not there.

I'm here, and clearly she and I are not done yet.

I think it's time we have that talk.

6

PERSEPHONE

God... I just touched myself, again.

As usual I was thinking about Lukiyan while I pleasured my body in the best ways I could. Except, seeing him again and having his name ring through my mind made me come harder than any other night.

Allowing the cold spray of water from the shower head to run down my body, I find respite in the coolness soothing the arousal burning deep within my skin.

It helps, but only somewhat.

My mind is still fucked.

I'm still aroused, and I'm still a mess because of him.

I have so many questions, they're falling out of my mind. But the most prevalent is how the hell he ended up here in New York working for my father.

Everything feels like a maddening mashup of a nightmare and a dream.

Like a ghost, Lukiyan's promise of *later* has haunted me all day.

Now, my anxiety has quadrupled, and there's not a soul I can speak to, to take the edge off my troubled mind.

Things were bad when all I had was Antonio to contend with, but with Lukiyan...

Well, he wasn't a problem, until now. I never thought I'd see him again.

What are the odds of having a one-night stand in Brazil and my guy showing up in New York, turning out to be my father's new bodyguard?

It's one hell of a coincidence.

I'd be inclined to think it was something more sinister, but I know it's not.

He didn't know who I was in Brazil. If he had, I'm sure he wouldn't have touched me.

Nevertheless, this entire occurrence is weird, and I can't pretend my problems away any more than I can that the heart beating in my chest is mine and not a parting gift from my sister.

Although I really can't imagine Lukiyan telling my father what happened

between us, I'm worried he might.

Since Mom and Athena died, my relationship with my father has been strained at best, and it's not because I hate his bitch wife who thinks she can take my mother's place. The reason is the mere fact that I live and breathe when I wasn't supposed to.

I already walk a thin line when it comes to my father

and it feels like he uses any excuse to punish me. This, however, would be my own fault.

I stand to gain nothing by telling anyone about Lukiyan. He, on the other

hand, could blackmail me, or rather, Father.

I wouldn't be the first daughter of a member of the Syndicate to lose their virginity.

Raven, for a start, lives the frivolous life of a playgirl Hollywood starlet. She sleeps around like she breathes air, and people know about it.

However, I'm not held to the same standards as everyone else. I'm judged at a higher bar simply for the fact that my father is on the Syndicate's council.

The members of the Syndicate are known as the Circle. There are ten founding families and twenty members of the High council.

The head of each founding family has a seat ranked in order of wealth and prestige. The remaining ten seats are reserved for members of the alliance of the same caliber.

My family was one of the founders and my father has the second seat on the council.

So the rules change for us when it comes to making an example. We don't get a pass because of power.

Which means now that Lukiyan Romanechka has stepped into my sphere of existence, I could be completely wrong in thinking I got away with losing my virginity.

What I did could blow up in my face and ruin my chances of escaping.

That would be worse than anything.

I turn off the shower and grab a towel from the rack to dry myself. Wrapping another around my body, I make my way back into my room like a mindless zombie.

I'm tired, but I don't know if sleep will come tonight.

I sink back onto the bed and slip my engagement ring in the drawer. I only wear it when I'm with Antonio.

When I straighten, I nearly jump out of my skin when I see a man standing by the window in the corner with the chiffon curtains billowing around him from the gentle breeze.

It's Lukiyan!

My God, he's in my room.

He's leaning against the wall, staring out the window as he smokes a cigarette.

How long has he been here?

What's he going to do to me?

A cacophony of emotions ravage my insides and I'm rooted to the spot, unable to move, unable to breathe, unable to think.

Clearly, now is *later.*

He turns to face me and makes a point of doing a full sweep of my body with those mystical eyes. He takes one last drag on his cigarette and puts it out.

"What are you doing in here?" My voice is raspy, as if I haven't spoken for a hundred years.

"It's later." He gives me that sexy half smile that does all sorts of things to my body.

"The door was locked." It was. I know I locked it.

"Not for me. You must have known I would come." His lips quirk into a little smile.

"I…" I don't know what to say. I practiced my answer all day. Now I can't think of a single thing that makes sense.

He comes closer, and my breath lodges in my throat.

"I never thought I was going to see you again." The words are tumbling from my mind.

He stops before me, wrapping me in his scent and raw masculinity.

Our eyes lock, and something sinful dances within the confines of his bright blue gaze.

"You and I have unfinished business."

"We do?"

"In Brazil you left my bed without saying goodbye, and I wasn't finished with you."

My throat goes dry, but every inch of my body heats up with wild arousal when he lowers his head like he's going to kiss me.

He doesn't, but stops a breath away from my lips, and his eyes rove up and down my body. It's then I remember all I have on is a towel.

"I… had to leave," I mutter.

"To run back to your fiancé? Yeah. I figured out that part."

"No, it wasn't like that. I don't love him." The explanation comes easy, but as the words tumble out of my mind, it strikes me that I shouldn't have said that.

I don't know him, and I've already opened myself to attack.

Lukiyan ignores my words and brushes his nose along mine.

The mere touch sends a jolt of electricity through my body, and I have to clench my thighs to contain the need aching inside me.

Jesus, all he did was touch me and look at me.

"Bad girls deserve to be punished."

"Punished?"

One dip of his head distracts me from the lightning-fast move he makes to secure a firm arm around my waist.

I swallow a scream when he lifts me higher onto the bed and secures a chain around my wrists, then hooks it into the rail of the wrought-iron headboard.

"What are you going to do to me?" I kick my legs, foolishly uncovering my body.

He chuckles, yanking the towel away from me so I'm lying there naked and exposed.

"Not sure yet." He flashes that deadly dimple on his left cheek when he smiles. "Maybe I should get you to touch yourself again the way you did earlier. You looked like you were having fun."

My eyes widen as I realize with humiliating horror that he was watching me.

He saw me touching myself. How, though? My bed isn't near the windows.

The cameras... there are cameras in here, but only my father has the password to gain access in emergencies.

Father has never had to use it since he installed them, which is why I thought I had privacy to do what I wanted.

So, what did Lukiyan do? Hack in?

Fuck. Of course, he did.

"You bastard," I snap, trying to get up. The restraints, however, hold me in place, reminding me that I'm not going anywhere.

When he looms over me, the fear I felt when we first said hello rushes back to me.

"I know what I want to start with."

Shrugging out of his jacket, he gets on the bed, and I gasp when he buries his face between my thighs.

My temperature spikes, and I feel like I'm standing next to the sun.

Lukiyan plunges his tongue into my pussy and... Oh. My. God!

Unimaginable pleasure races over my body, and I can't believe I forgot how good this felt—him tasting me, eating my pussy as if he wants to devour me forever.

I made myself forget because of the torture of remembering and knowing I wouldn't be able to relive the fantasy.

But look at me.

He's here.

I was trying not to show the impact of the pleasure, but I can't.

His tongue licks and swirls around my clit, tugging on the nub and nipping at it with his teeth. He thrusts deeper and deeper, swirling around the edges of my outer lips, and I cum on his face, losing my mind.

I cry out from the sensation and moan loudly when he slides his hands up my body and cups my breasts.

Kneading both, he continues to eat me out, then he moves to my asshole to lick me there as I lift my hips.

He thrusts his tongue inside there, too, then stops and watches me with a wild smile on his face.

The smile is one of victory. As if he knows he's tapped into something deep inside me that only he can reach.

I know what it is.

There were some parts of that night in Brazil that were darker than I wanted to acknowledge. We had anal sex, he spanked me, almost choked me, and we were rough.

He was rough with me and dirty. There were parts that hurt, which I shouldn't have liked as much as I did, and I never stopped him.

Now I'm chained to my bed, and I'm having the same problem.

From the foreboding look in his eyes, I know we're both thinking of the same things.

I should scream for help. Even though I know no one will hear me, at least the scream would be some act of defiance to save myself. It would be something to show him I don't want him.

But all I'm doing is lying here soaking up the pleasure.

"Bad girl indeed," he mutters, moving up to my breasts.

He sucks my tight, taut nipples hard but slow, and that feels good too.

"Do you want more, Princess?"

"Y...essss," I moan.

"Beg me. Beg me to give you more pleasure."

I want to tell him that I won't beg for anything, but the devil knows best.

He moves back to my pussy and slams one finger into my passage, sending me spinning into ecstasy again.

"Please," I cry. "Please, give me more pleasure."

I can't believe I'm saying those words, but the desperation sweeping through me makes me believe I'll die if he doesn't give me more.

With a wicked smile, he returns to my breasts and sucks one then the other until my nipples are sore.

He kisses his way back down to my pussy, and the moment his lips brush over my mound, I come. *Hard.*

I come so hard I arch off the bed, rubbing my pussy against his face.

"Say my name, Princess." Menace taints his smile.

"Lukiyan!"

"Good girl."

He comes back to my lips, and we kiss, cruel and ravishing as if we can't get enough of each other.

Feeling his hard length pressing into my belly, I crave it.

Is he going to fuck me?

Would I really allow him to take me like this?

What choice do I have?

I can't move even if I want to.

I'm whisked from my thoughts when he pulls away

and stands on the bed so he can shove his pants down his hips.

"Now, open your mouth and suck my dick."

My mouth falls open, salivating to suck him. He moves right up to my face with his fully-erect cock, and like the brute he is, he grabs a fist of my hair and shoves his cock into my mouth.

He starts fucking my mouth with a brutal force. It's angry and so violent I wonder if this is the real punishment for not telling him who I was.

With a strained but pleasure-filled look on his handsome face, he mutters something in what I think is Russian. In fact, I'm certain it is. I just have no idea what he's saying, only that he sounds sexy and arousing.

Lukiyan continues speaking in Russian and surprises me when he strokes the top of my head. The language sounds like sweet nothings, like pure desire, like the magic working its way into my soul.

Then he speeds up making me gag. Tears stream from the corners of my eyes as I take his relentless pounds.

He sees my struggle but forces me to suck him harder and faster, bobbing my head up and down. His cock stiffens in my mouth, and from the growl that rips out of his throat, I sense he's coming. Seconds later, he does, but he pulls out of my mouth and his cum spurts over my face. It pours out of his cock as he fists his length, making sure every last drop reaches me.

It's warm on my skin and sticky. Lines of it flow on to my lips and down my neck.

"Clean up the rest and swallow it," he commands pushing his cock back to my mouth.

Like a mindless slave, I lean forward and lick the remnants of cum off his cock.

When I swallow, he smiles with satisfaction and I hate the way my body reacts at the sight of his stupid dimples.

He bends down and comes close to my ear in a predatory manner. "This meeting never happened. Just like Brazil."

Never happened?

Suddenly I'm pulled back to reality as I realize what he's saying to me. I take it to mean we're good when it comes to our secret meeting in Brazil, but deep down I'm hurt and I can't ignore the pang that grips my heart.

How exactly am I supposed to forget I lost my virginity to him?

Never happened.

Except it did. *We* did.

"Do you understand me, Persephone Vittorio?" he says my name like he's trying it out. "Understand?" His voice is harsher, scarier.

"I understand." Although I speak, my voice sounds like it's coming from far away.

"Good girl. We never happened. Except..." His smile becomes wicked and full of menace. "Every time you're with your *beloved fiancé*, you'll always remember the scent of me, and how I taste. You'll always remember that I had you first. And, I still have you....*Princess.*"

Lukiyan plants a kiss on my chest and lingers by the

tattoo masking my scar. He feels over the design, making a point of feeling over the slightly-raised skin on the scar of my deep wound, like he wants me to know he's aware of what's there.

Another kiss is left there along with a tingle which makes me feel... *alive.*

It's strange.

Why would I feel alive when I should be disgusted with myself?

Any dignity I previously had is gone.

He moves away, tucks his cock back into his pants, and releases my restraints. One last look, and he leaves.

The door swings shut with a final click behind him, and I'm left on the bed with his cum all over me, his scent clinging to my skin like a stamp of ownership.

Even though this meeting never happened, it doesn't feel like he's finished with me.

It feels like he's only just begun.

7

LUKIYAN

It didn't work.

I didn't get Persephone Vittorio out of my system.

She's still in there screwing with my mind in the most decadent of ways, and I'm still fucked.

What I should have done is fucked her.

Fuck her one last time and satisfy the craving she's given me.

I could have, but I didn't because I knew she'd ruin me.

She'd push me over that line to obsession, and I'd want her more than I already do.

Last night I knew I shouldn't have allowed desire to get the better of me, and I should have left well enough alone. But I also know I would do the same thing all over again if given the choice.

Now I have to live with the consequences of my actions.

It's a new day with a new set of challenges.

I arrived at the Grand Vittorio at eight a.m. sharp to start my first official day on the job. This is the flagship hotel in Emilio's empire.

Two bulky-looking guards who look like they served in the Marines searched me on entry. Daily searches are standard protocol even though I'm part of the crew.

Smart move. Protocols like that keep people on edge and alert.

I've been standing in the lobby between the restaurant and the casino for the last four hours watching the place.

It's been years since I had a job where I practically do nothing but observe.

I'm treating it like my stakeout sessions where I'm tracking my next kill.

So far the only activity has been the people leaving the restaurant and the excitement in the casino.

There's already been a fight where two drunks battling it out over a woman had to be escorted off the premises.

What it's been is normal, which feels abnormal for me.

Watching regular people walk into a place that is owned by darkness is strange.

I have a change of scenery in a few minutes when I'll head up to the tenth floor, then a break after, which I'm going to use to get some air.

The parts of this mission that require my patience are driving me more insane than I already am.

When I'm left to my thoughts like this, Persephone enters my mind. She's complicated things for me. Having her stuck in my head has jarred my brain and my body.

The look on her face as I ran my finger over her scar stayed with me too, and I want to know what caused it. There are only a few things that can cause a scar like that —the ones that never truly fade, even when they become invisible to the eye.

As if on cue, she materializes in front of me.

She walks into the lobby with Raven. They are followed by her aunt—Raven's mother, and her step-mother who are practically walking arm in arm as they talk excitedly. Antonio is behind them.

I didn't know Persephone was going to be here today, and she clearly didn't know I was either.

Her autumn-colored eyes round when they see me, filling with fear, arousal and curiosity.

Raven looks at me too, but it's the way most women do —like they want to fuck me.

Persephone's aunt and stepmother don't even acknowledge my existence.

Antonio, on the other hand, does, and he's definitely pissed that his fiancée is looking at me the way she is.

He ushers the women into the restaurant and doubles back, heading my way.

As he approaches, I remember what Persephone said— that she didn't love him.

Hearing it was nice, even though it was something I'd already figured out.

I knew their marriage was arranged before Emilio told me Persephone was promised to Antonio.

"Lukiyan Romanechka." Antonio beams, stopping a few paces away.

"That is me." I keep my tone even.

He straightens and squares his shoulders. We're the same height but not the same build, so when I set my shoulders back, they look wider than his.

He thinks I'm a simple bodyguard—a minion, a runt, a new guy he can push around. Little does he know I could kill him with my bare hands before he takes his next breath. I'm sure he could give me a good fight. He has the muscle, but I'd win.

"We didn't get a chance to talk properly yesterday," he begins. "Since I'm going to be away for a few days, I thought I'd take the chance to have a word."

"Oh, yeah?"

"Yes. I like to know who's who and what everyone is doing. Especially now that I'll be in charge of the security team when I marry Persephone."

This fool must like the sound of his own voice.

I know why he wants to talk to me, and it's not to tell me about his upcoming endeavors or chat like we're pals.

"What do you want to know about me?" I would so love to give him a firsthand experience of who I really am.

"It's more like I wanted to tell you something."

"What?"

His eyes squint, and there's a tick in his jaw giving his calm away. "Keep your eyes off my woman."

There it is.

I can't help but smile. "Keep my eyes off your woman? What, are we in high school?"

"You heard me." Antonio gives me a holier-than-thou smirk. "Try to remember she's mine. Got it?"

My blood simmers like a pressure cooker waiting to explode as he steps into my personal space. I nearly lose my shit when he reaches out and brushes invisible lint off my jacket. His fake smile widens, and I want to pull my knife and cut it off his face. The last guy who made the mistake of touching me like this is now six feet under. I sliced him up six ways to Sunday.

I want to do that now.

But I can't.

I shouldn't.

Mustn't.

I have to play the game. *For Melissa.* Only for Melissa.

"I got it," I grate out.

"Good."

He shoves me hard in my chest and grins. At the same time, the doors open, and Frankie and Emilio walk in.

"Hey, cut it out," Frankie states with furrowed brows.

Emilio doesn't comment. All he does is eye me with caution. Both he and Frankie would have seen what Antonio did, and they probably guessed his reasons too, although I've barely had any interaction with Persephone to get them worked up.

If they'd seen the way she sucked my cock last night and watched me eat out her pussy, I could understand.

The three continue into the restaurant, and I watch them sit at the long table.

Persephone is already looking at me when I switch my focus to her.

Antonio thinks she belongs to him.

She doesn't.

How can she when she feels like mine?

I can't stop wanting her, and it doesn't look like the princess wants me to stop either.

8

PERSEPHONE

I take a breath of the cool air and allow it to cleanse my lungs and my head.

I'm sitting on a bench in the rose garden just outside the hotel restaurant taking a much-needed break.

Everyone is still inside. The men are talking business, Alecia and Aunt Marissa were absorbed with planning their next charity event, and Raven was texting someone. Or more like sexting.

I managed to slip away after the dessert I didn't want and retreat out here where I could think and regroup after seeing Lukiyan.

I didn't know he was going to be here today, but there's no surprise really. He's supposed to do the same job as everyone else, so why wouldn't he be here?

Seeing him again so soon was just unexpected.

I can still feel the strength of his gaze on me. It was as

potent and brutal as his touch was last night, accompanied with the reminder that we never happened.

I didn't sleep after our wild encounter. So, now exhaustion has worked its way into every inch of my body.

I hardly had the strength to walk into the restaurant and pretend that seeing him again didn't shatter my world. Or remind me of the sweet nothings he spoke to me in Russian and that I was covered in his cum.

I can't believe that was us. I had his cock in my mouth again, and the way he punished my mouth left me spent yet aching for more.

More of what I shouldn't want.

Now I have to live through the rest of today.

My family and I are going to the church in a little while to meet the priest who's supposed to conduct the wedding ceremony.

I'm going through the motions only because I know I won't be following through on the real thing and because falling in line allows me small doses of freedom.

I'm coming back here later to dance. I practice at home, but it's not the same as using the stage in the theater here. I've been doing that every day for the last few months.

It's undoubtedly been the only thing to save me from going *One Flew Over the Cuckoo's Nest* crazy.

"There you are," Raven says, cutting into my thoughts.

She rounds the corner and slides up next to me with a little smile.

"Please don't tell me they're summoning me back in."
My shoulders slump.

"No, not yet." She breathes out a heavy sigh and tucks a
lock of her hair behind her ear.

"Thank God. I can't go back inside yet." Not with
Antonio grabbing my leg under the table and trying to feel
his way up to my panties.

I saw him talking to Lukiyan. I don't know what he
said, but I don't think it was anything good.

Raven rests a comforting hand on my shoulder. "I
would have come out here before to check on you, but I
thought you might need some time to yourself."

My cousin is one of the few people left in this world
who truly know me.

"I did, but I'm glad you're here."

Mischief lights up her eyes as she reaches into her bag,
pulls out a little roll-up and hands it to me. It's a joint. If
anyone caught us with it, we'd be so dead.

Raven gets away with all sorts of things. She keeps me
in touch with the outside world.

"Thought you might need this."

"I do."

She takes out a lighter and lights the end for me. When
I take a drag, calmness soothes me.

"Feel better?"

"No, but I guess my head doesn't feel like it's going to
explode anymore."

"Talk to me." Her eyes fill with concern.

"It's best I don't." I shake my head and breathe deeper,

wishing I could talk to her about everything. Like Lukiyan and my escape plans.

But I can't. I can't talk to her about either, especially the latter.

Not only will her knowledge of my plan jeopardize my escape, but it will undoubtedly get her in trouble too. My father is a ruthless man who's known for his savage ways. While he holds his family close to his heart, that doesn't mean he'll be hesitant to dole out punishment. If the crime fits, it won't matter who you are to him.

The person helping me is Maya, my former nanny and head maid in our household. She's been looking after me since I was born.

She's Brazilian and worked for my mother's family before my parents got married.

She witnessed Antonio's aggression toward me months ago and became my savior when she offered to help me escape.

She's been my only hope of freedom in this mess.

If she succeeds in getting what I need to leave, it means all will go to plan at the fundraiser.

My father probably trusts her more than anyone. I trust her the same way, so I know she won't let me down.

She begged me to keep the plan between us, and I have. We've been planning between ourselves and gotten this far. I know, though, that if I make it out, everything is going to be much harder. I'll be on my own then and won't have anyone to turn to.

"Fuck knows who they'll marry me off to." Raven gives me a weary smile.

"Let's hope it's someone nice." I pray my absence won't mean she'll have to marry Antonio.

I doubt that since Raven won't be inheriting the empire.

With me gone, it will go to Frankie. It's weird the way our inheritance works. It stays with the eldest family member and their heirs before it jumps to their siblings.

"So, I kind of saw the new bodyguard looking at you," she states with a saucy smile. "And I saw you looking at him, too."

God, I can't have this conversation with her now. I already feel bad she still thinks I'm a virgin. When she lost hers, she told me, and I always planned to tell her when my time came.

Athena and I were scarily close and had that shared twin mind people talk about, but Raven has always been my best friend. It's hurting me that I have to keep my secrets from her, but it's hurting more that after Friday, I won't be able to see her ever again.

"I just happened to see him."

She smirks. "Are you kidding me? You didn't just happen to see him. The man is fucking hot, and he looked at you like he wanted to fuck you."

My body heats at the mention of fucking.

If she knew that I, Miss Goody-Two-Shoes, had a one-night stand with the hottest man I could find in a night club, her head would implode.

"I'm sure it's just you who thought that."

"No, it wasn't, and Antonio totally saw too. I'm certain he said something to him about it."

I think he did too.

"Like what?"

"Who cares? I saw the way Lukiyan looked at you. If I were you, I'd work that and let him do whatever he wants to me."

I wish I could tell her I already have. "You know I can't."

"Oh, please, you know Antonio is getting it from any nubile girl who'll ride his dick."

"I know."

"All the more reason to ride that stallion, or whatever Lukiyan is. I can't figure him out other than the fact that he's hot."

She can join the club. Although I think I know a little more than her in the department of figuring Lukiyan out —as in one little thing. I think he has some Russian in him. He doesn't look it, but the way he spoke Russian to me felt like it was as commonplace to him as English. I'm not even like that with Italian or Portuguese, and I've always been encouraged to speak both.

"At least he would keep your mind off things." She chuckles. "He's pretty to look at, and you could do stuff. Wild sexy stuff."

Like last night?

No, thanks. Even as I think that, the hunger inside me clings to the memory of being devoured and desired.

"Raven, I can't do that."

"Just remember I gave you the green light. I love anything that rubs Antonio the wrong way. I wanted better for you, even more than I do for myself."

She gives my hand a gentle squeeze.

"Thank you." I feel like a hypocrite sitting here with an exit strategy and not sharing it with her.

"I miss the old days." She gives me a reminiscent smile. "We'd be getting ready to go to Brazil again in a few weeks."

I smile at the memory. "I miss those days, too."

When I was little, we'd all go to Brazil three times a year.

We only go there now because Father owns Mom's family business. When we see family, it's brief. But it's something. That's why I was so excited to go on that last trip.

I have to say goodbye to that, too. I won't be able to see that side of my family ever again, and my *avó* —my grandmother—is getting old and frail. I was hoping to see her again before she dies.

"Maybe we can have those days again."

We can't, but I'll humor her.

"Maybe."

9

LUKIYAN

Tell me not to do something, and I'll do it a million times.

It's the rebel in me.

My nature is to defy and follow my own desires and instincts.

That's what led me here to the hotel's theater, where I found myself watching the princess dance to Debussy's *Clair de Lune*.

She's doing ballet.

I've blended in with the shadows so she can't see me.

This—dancing here by herself when the theater is free, seems to be something she does regularly.

I was making my last rounds of the hotel for the day when I found her.

The music she's dancing to is the kind of music my father used to play all the time, especially when we trained. He always had on classical pieces like Bach and Debussy—music that speaks directly to the soul.

Music that has the ability to make you feel alive and at the same time take life in the art of death.

I should have guessed she was a dancer from the way she moved at the club in Brazil. I never figured her for ballet though. Not that it doesn't suit her.

It does. It suits her more than anything, and she has raw talent accompanied by skill.

It's just that although she has the grace of a swan, her body looks more athletic than willowy like most dancers I've come across.

Put simply, she has a body made for fucking and the kind of debauchery my devilish mind can conjure.

The black sleeveless leotard she's wearing only serves to illustrate my point perfectly. The eroticized vision of her is only tamed to a meager extent by the light pink chiffon skirt flowing around her hips.

The way she moves, twirling and leaping across the stage, shows she was born to dance. She moves as if she's a part of the music. As if they are one and the same.

Both have had me rooted to this spot on the second-floor balcony for the last hour.

I wonder if this was what happened to Hades when he first became obsessed with Persephone. Did he watch her for hours on end getting lost in time before he stole her?

Did he ever think he would lose himself the way he did?

He knew exactly where to find the maiden when she was gathering flowers on that plain in Sicily. When he appeared in all his glory, in his four-horse chariot from hell, he planned her theft with such efficacy, not a soul knew when he struck until after it happened.

It's curious and odd for the God of the Underworld to succumb to love, but that was something more sinister than love.

Love is patient, love is kind. It does not envy, it does not boast, it is not proud. It does not dishonor others, it is not self-seeking, it is not easily angered, it keeps no record of wrongs. Love does not delight in evil...

Hades acted with obsession, not love.

Love came after, when he allowed his maiden to see the light.

My maiden and her music have soothed the beast inside me that's always raging to kill, kill, kill and satisfy my thirst for revenge.

The beast resided in my dark soul long before Melissa died.

The creature has always been fueled with rage because I felt that life dropped me in the deep end of the ocean and expected me to learn to swim in shark-infested waters.

Persephone leaps through the air again as the intensity of the music heightens and I'm reminded of the last ballet my birth mother took me to.

It was she who introduced me to the world of classical music and dance.

She loved ballet and loved this piece of music in

particular. When she taught me how to play the piano, this was the piece I first learned.

She did ballet briefly when she was a little girl and learned to play the piano. Her parents were too poor for her to continue lessons.

Even when we were in Russia, Mom would take Melissa and me to the opera and the ballet. She'd even sneak us in when we couldn't afford it.

Those memories are some of the only good ones I have of her—the more peaceful ones.

The ones that didn't see her high on crack or battered after a run-in with one of her many boyfriends who loved to show her the end of their fist.

I never knew who my birth father was. All I know about him is that he was Italian. I assumed he was in the mafia from some of the things Mom told me. She was always vague and sad when she talked about him.

She was a student when she met him and she dropped out of school when she got pregnant with me. She never specifically said this, but I think my real father was married and had an affair with her.

When I first met my adopted father, it was the music that made me trust him. It felt like a piece of my past I could rely on. Even though the only thing I could trust about my real mother was that she loved me and wanted to keep my sister and me safe.

The music slows, coming to the end of the piece, and I straighten, readying to leave because I should. However, when I think of leaving without getting closer to Persephone, my mind shuns the idea.

I don't know what the hell it is about this woman that's gotten to me and loosened my iron-clad control, but I find myself making my way down to the stage against my better judgment.

I take the little steps leading up and wait by the curtains until the music stops and she turns into one last pirouette then curtseys as if she'd performed for a full audience. Not just me.

She stays in that curtsey for a few moments, as though savoring the feel of it.

It's not until she lifts her head that she sees me and she moves out of the position, staring at me with a deer-caught-in-the-headlights expression.

Her full lips part, and an elegant flush of crimson skates over her pale cheeks and down the silky skin of her neck.

Panic and fear invade her beautiful eyes, as they should.

She's right to be alarmed by my presence.

There is nothing good in me and nothing good to expect from me if I'm planning to kill her father.

Aside from that, the number of sexual encounters we've had vastly outweighs what can be expected for strangers.

The first night we met, we'd barely known each other for an hour before I was balls deep inside her. I had her three times that night and would have kept going if she hadn't passed out. Not to mention, I owned her ass, too.

So yeah, that look on her face is a sea of emotions clashing together like a tempestuous storm.

"I didn't know you were there." Her voice comes out in a rasp while her chest rises and falls like she's out of breath.

That's not from dancing. It's from the quickening of her heart at the sight of me.

"Because I didn't let you know until I wanted to."

I move closer, stopping a breath away, and I'm reminded of how tiny she is.

With a lift of her chin, she seems to find her courage. She folds her arms under her breasts and stares at me head on, her gaze unwavering.

"Are you here to screw with me again?" Her throat works as she swallows hard.

"Do you want me to?"

"Does that even warrant an answer?"

A hint of a genuine smile twists my lips, a record for me considering few things truly amuse me. Normally when I smile, it's to intimidate. "I think it does."

"I don't." She glares at me with undiluted distaste.

"Don't worry, this meeting won't end with my cock in your mouth again." My venomous words make her recoil, taking a few steps back. "That is, not unless you want it. I certainly wouldn't say no."

"Could you be more arrogant?"

"Yes, but then you wouldn't like me as much as you do."

She smirks without humor. "I don't like you."

The incensed press of her lips and the blaze in her eyes are supposed to support what she's saying, but her body betrays her, telling a different story.

From the state of her diamond-hard nipples to the dilation of her pupils, I know she's fighting a losing battle.

She likes me well enough, and I'm sure by now it's no secret that I like her too.

I lean in, and she lifts her head higher so we're eye to eye. "I'd believe you a lot more if your tits didn't look hard enough to cut glass."

"You're an asshole. A complete jerk after what you did to me, and if you think I like that, you're surely mistaken."

I love the fire that's suddenly entered her eyes. It reminds me of what attracted me to her when we first met. The woman I met in Brazil was the real her. She was wild and reckless as hell. Knowing who she is now, I know the risks she took that night. But part of me loves that she did it anyway to taste freedom.

I like the whole package, but I want that woman back. Nobody but me got to see her that way.

She was herself when she was with me.

"I don't think I'm mistaken," I say, infuriating her even more.

"What do you want?" Her pulse throbs at the side of her throat as she attempts to imbue her voice with confidence, but the quiver lacing through her words lets her down. "I thought you said we never happened."

I did say that, and I should go with the plan I first hatched, but nothing about Persephone Vittorio is following my rules.

"If you're here to make sure I don't talk about Brazil, you don't have to worry about that." She brings her hands together. "I'm not saying anything to anyone. Do I have to worry about you?"

Of course, she's still worried I might do that.

"No." I keep my tone even as I observe relief enter her taut expression.

She blinks and releases a deep sigh, which causes her tits to lift. The sight makes my dick fill with blood, and I want to suck on her nipples again to hear her moans of pleasure.

My eyes rove up and down her body, and the tension returns to her face.

"Thank you."

She shouldn't thank me. I'm her worst enemy, and when she finds out, she'll despise me.

"Where did you learn to dance like that?" I change the subject because we need to.

"I'm a dancer. Or... rather I *was* one. I've been dancing all my life." She presses her lips together.

"Why was?"

"I..." Her voice trails off as she thinks about her next words. "With my upcoming marriage to Antonio, I'm not going to be allowed to do it anymore. I went to Juilliard."

Even I'm impressed to hear that, but not surprised after watching her.

"I didn't finish," she adds.

"Sorry to hear that. You're very talented." I never compliment anybody unless they truly deserve it, and even then, I'm not the guy to issue praise easily.

A twinkle flashes in her eyes, making my dance around my rules totally worth it.

"I appreciate that." She studies my face, and when curiosity fills her eyes, I know she's going to want to know about me next. "Where did you come from, Lukiyan?"

I lean in again. "Maybe it's best if you don't know."

"Why would that be best? It's a big coincidence that you're here, don't you think?"

"Yes."

"Was it … a coincidence?"

"It was."

Her features soften, slowly loosening her up almost to how she was in Brazil. "That makes me want to know who you are even more."

I couldn't tell her that even if I weren't keeping my identity a secret. So I decide to give her an answer to make her think.

"I'm your Hades," I say.

She'll know what I mean by that. The blush creeping into her cheeks again tells me she does, and although I remind myself of where my focus should lie, it doesn't eradicate my desire to be inside her again.

Her lips part as if she's going to comment, but the words don't come. Instead, her gaze lifts past my shoulder and she looks up at something with trepidation in her eyes.

I follow her gaze and find her old man standing on the highest balcony, watching us. Dressed in full black, he looks like he's part of the mass of shadows behind him.

Persephone steps away from me and dips her head.

"I have to go now," she stutters, then turns on her heel and leaves.

I'm taking risks I shouldn't take and asking to get my ass fired. I was warned to keep my dick in my pants, and look at me.

Returning my gaze to Emilio, I catch the hard stare he casts my way and the unspoken warning before he turns and leaves, disappearing into the shadows.

I know the risks and how important being here is to me, but my recklessness isn't about that.

It's about her—Persephone.

I can't resist the lure that draws me to her because she's the kind of woman who makes men like me drop their guard.

She's the kind of woman who makes a man think of all he would do to own her, possess her, and make her his forever.

She's the kind of woman to steal your heart and soul.

I think that's what happened to Hades.

It wasn't the other way around.

It was Persephone who ruined him.

The image of my sister lying dead on the floor of her room fills my mind, along with that final doom I felt when I knew I couldn't save her.

This is the only thing I can do for her, and I can't allow anyone to stand in the way.

That needs to include Persephone too.

10

PERSEPHONE

I am your Hades.

Lukiyan's words delivered the intended blow.

They've been stuck on repeat in my mind. I haven't stopped thinking about them, or him, and I wonder what exactly he meant.

That he'd take me away the way Hades stole Persephone?

That he was fascinated with me?

That he was as drawn to me as I am to him?

I don't know, but I'd be a liar if I said my knees didn't weaken and my heart didn't speed up.

I'd also be a fool to entertain these feelings.

Still, it was nice to feel alive again for those few moments and be swept back to the mythical stories Mom used to tell me when I was little.

She loved Greek mythology. That's why she named her twins Athena and Persephone.

Mom told us our names matched our personalities. Athena was the artist just like our mother, and I was the dancer. The lover of life and living.

I remember when I first heard the story of Hades and Persephone. I used to always imagine falling in love with someone I couldn't live without.

Just like how Persephone fell for Hades, God of the Underworld. I can see Lukiyan being him.

He's dark and twisted that way. But so am I, in other ways because I already know what it's like to live in the underworld.

Sometimes I wonder if hell is calling for me to come home, except I never know why I feel like I'm deserving of hell and not heaven's gates.

Maybe it's because of what I'm doing now.

I'm being selfish. Completely and utterly selfishly taking control of my life.

As I make my way down the dark corridor, I swear I feel Lukiyan's eyes on me again.

The sensation is so overpowering I glance behind me. But he isn't there; there's no one there. Just the shadows.

I'm officially paranoid now, and I have every reason to be because I'm terrified I'll get caught.

It's five fifteen in the morning, and I'm going to meet Maya to get the last of the things I need for my plans on Friday.

Two more days, then I'm gone. On Saturday morning, I should be on my way to England.

Right now, I just have to focus on putting one foot in

front of the other and shove away the uncanny thought away that Lukiyan is watching me.

He can't see you, Persephone.

No one can.

Only the ghosts.

There are no cameras on this side of the house, and it's only lit by moonlight.

This side doesn't have the automatic lights that turn on like in the rest of the house. Father didn't install those over here because he restricted access to everyone after the massacre.

This was where it all happened.

Sometimes I wished we'd moved after, but my father has some unusual ways of doing things.

I think he stayed because he believes my mother is still here, and so is Athena.

The rustling wind flows through the windows, making them chatter like teeth on edge, and the sound of nothingness is almost deafening.

Sometimes when I'm here, I hear more noises than I know should be here.

The faint cry of a baby who no longer exists.

Athena's soft laughter.

The dulcet tone of my mother's voice telling us stories of the gods of Olympus and their goddesses.

Mom's voice—even if it's inside my head—is the one that soothes me the most.

Our lives were full of happiness when Mom was alive. My father was a different man then.

He was so in love with her. She was the calm to his storm. The light in his dark world.

His heartbeat.

I used to pray for love like that.

When she died, he died too.

And so did I.

I always feel guilty that he blames me for her death because he couldn't get to her in time. I was so sick that day, all everyone thought of was getting me to safety when we heard the sounds of gunfire and screaming. I couldn't even walk, so she practically carried me. Athena helped, and it was to her detriment too.

That day ruined her just as much as death could have. After what happened to her, she was never herself again.

That day, we lost our mother, but we lost her, too.

The floorboards creak under my feet as I walk into the old hall.

This room is the most haunted section of the house. It was where Mom was killed along with five other members of staff.

The creak of another set of footsteps makes my nerves spike, but I calm when Maya steps out from behind one of the long mirrors.

Like me, she's dressed in black, in a long coat that looks more like a robe.

She rushes to me with arms stretched wide and holds me the way Mom used to. At forty-two years old, she's much younger than my mother was when she died, but in these moments, she offers the motherly comfort I yearn for.

When she pulls away, she smiles, and I take that as a good sign.

"I got what you need." She keeps her voice low, speaking with a hint of a Brazilian accent, which makes me feel like I'm there again.

I bring my hands to my cheeks and try to hold back the tears of joy threatening to pour out of me.

"I'm really going to be able to leave?"

"Yes. Here, take this." She reaches into her pocket and pulls out a little brown envelope. "Inside is your new I.D. You've got a new birth certificate and passport. There's also a credit card with the remaining two grand on it."

I take the packet and hug her again. "Thank you so much."

That two grand is all I have left to start my new life.

Maya is a sweet soul who has connections and people who will do anything for her. So what could have cost me close to half a million only cost ten grand.

I have a substantial allowance and a trust fund which Father keeps an eye on. So I had to withdraw small amounts of money at a time and sell off jewelry I didn't want to sell that my *avó* gave it to me.

"No need to thank me, sweet girl. I honestly don't believe your mother would be happy to see you in such distress and with a man like Antonio. I also don't think she'd be very happy with me if I didn't help you."

"Thank you so, so very much. Please tell me you'll be okay. I don't want you to get in trouble."

"I won't. When you've been around for as long as I have, you know how to cover yourself. So do not worry about me. Okay?"

"Okay."

She cups my face and smiles wide and proud. "I will miss you terribly, but it has to be this way. You know what to do now."

I nod. "Get on the boat on Friday night and don't look back."

"Don't look back. It will break your heart."

My heart.

No, not mine. Never mine. My heart is dead.

She means my sister's heart.

It was a gift and a sacrifice. One I don't take lightly.

Under no circumstances will I dishonor that or allow anyone else to break me.

That's why I'm doing what I'm doing.

Hours later I make my way into the breakfast room, where I find my father reading the morning paper.

On the long mahogany table is the exquisite breakfast Porsha has made for us. She's standing next to Father, pouring his coffee.

Like Maya, she's worked for us since I was born, and I think she'll be serving my father until the day she dies.

I get on with her when she's not talking about me behind my back.

Porsha doesn't like my attitude toward Antonio and his family. She's one of those women who thinks the sun shines from their asses and I should feel more grateful I got Antonio.

I don't care what she thinks any more than I do for the stiff smile she issues me.

I was going to skip breakfast today but thought better of it because it will be the last one I have with my father.

He's traveling later on one of his many business trips, so I won't see him until the fundraiser. Then he'll be too busy with his associates to notice me, and I'll be too busy with my escape plan.

There are a few things I want to talk to him about.

I want to have that heart-to-heart we never got to have about this so-called wedding. Knowing I'm leaving has given me a boost of power and strength to confront him.

Aside from that, this will be my goodbye. I don't want to leave without talking to him properly.

We drove back home in silence last night after he saw me talking to Lukiyan. I was waiting for him to pull me up about that, but he didn't.

He didn't say anything at all, which was worse than our usual arguments where he lays down the law and I follow orders.

Despite everything that's happened, I still love my father with all my heart. I just wish he could love me the same way and that he didn't blame me for the losses we've had in our lives.

"Buongiorno, Persephone. Would you like some tea?" Porsha asks.

"Sì grazie. Some Jasmine tea will be great."

"Of course."

She pours me a cup then saunters through the double oak doors leading to the kitchen, leaving me with Father, who is staring at me.

He doesn't have his patch on today, so I can see his damaged eye. Sometimes, it's jarring to look at him this way.

When he had both eyes, they were so vibrant and full of magic that his smile would reach them and his entire face would light up.

He used to look like a person, not a killer.

Those were the days when Mom would be the one making breakfast and baking cookies for later.

Now we have this, and that eye looks like it's always judging me, even though there's no life in it. Deep down, I think Father blames me for that too.

In a way, it was my fault. If he didn't need to save me, he'd still have both eyes. And maybe Mom would still be alive. That would mean Athena would have lived as well. I think so, anyway.

In fact, I know so.

"Buongiorno, Father." I speak first because he's still looking at me.

"Buongiorno."

"Are you okay?" I bring my hands together so he can't see the tremor. I'm nervous for so many reasons.

"I'm fine," he states, still giving me that hard stare. "While we're alone, I'd like to talk to you about Antonio,"

"Why?" *What the hell now?* I pray it's not some shit that will push me over the edge before Friday.

"I don't like the way you are with Antonio. It's always clear you don't want to marry him."

"Because I don't." I try to say that in the calmest voice possible.

Father's nostrils flare. "It's going to happen, Persephone, whether you like it or not."

No, it's not.

I want to scream the words but restrain myself.

I know he'll hate me even more when he discovers I'm gone, but I can't worry about that now.

"Why didn't you tell me about Antonio before?" I take the chance to jump right into what I've been dying to ask for the last few months. "You knew you were going to marry me off to him. Why did you allow me to go to Juilliard and work so hard to get picked for the collaboration with the New York City Ballet? Why when you knew it was never going to happen?"

"Things happen, Persephone. Life happens. And sometimes, changes happen beyond our control."

"But this was in your control, Father. You're second-in-command in the Camorra and the don of the New York outfit. You could have done anything you wanted, but you did this."

I've never spoken to him like this before, and I'm not even showing an ounce of the anger I truly feel. Out of respect and love, I'm holding back.

"You don't get to question my authority or decisions."

"What about love, Papa?" I used to call him that when I was little.

It's the first time in many years that I've done so. Maybe I just want to hear myself say it one last time.

He tenses, his back going straight and his features hardening even more.

"I gave up on love when I lost your mother." Which means he doesn't love Alecia.

I could almost rejoice at his answer because I hate Alecia with all my heart. I hate the way she waltzed into our lives and took over. But there's nothing to rejoice because she has more of my father's heart than I do.

"I never gave up on love. Mom wouldn't have wanted me to. You know that, so it feels like you're punishing me."

He holds my stare for a few moments, and I almost think he's not going to say anything more.

"This is your duty. It's not about punishment—"

"I love you, Papa," I cut in before he can continue. "I remember when we used to say that to each other every day. Now you can barely stand to look at me. So do not sit there and tell me you aren't punishing me. Sometimes, I think you wish I'd died."

This is his chance to tell me I'm wrong.

I just want to hear him say those words, and I'll be okay.

Instead of feeling like I shouldn't be living, I'll remember him telling me he loves me, and I'm completely mistaken to believe anything else.

But he doesn't correct me.

He gives me that emotionless stare, and I know I'm not going to hear the words I've longed for.

"You need to focus on the wedding," he says, and as the words fall from his lips, my heart breaks. "Remember you're going to be a wife. That means whatever fascination you have with the new bodyguard ends here."

At that moment, Porsha returns with Alecia in tow, looking like the lady of the manor.

She plants herself down next to Father, and it's like our conversation never happened.

The only thing left hanging in the air is my father's warning and the emptiness I've felt inside since I got my borrowed life.

11

LUKIYAN

"What about you, handsome? Don't you want a drink? Or something else?" asks the topless waitress standing before me, wearing a barely-there electric pink thong.

When I hesitate with my answer, her smile turns up a notch and she tilts her head to the side, allowing her long platinum waves to fall over her shoulder.

"No, I'm good."

"Are you sure?" She steps closer, and her puckered nipples brush my suit jacket.

"I'm very sure."

I'm used to this. It's part of my world, and the woman before me is exactly my type.

I'm working, she knows I am, but all the men here— the guards included—have been offered a woman of their choosing for the night.

This woman clocked on me the moment I started my shift.

I'm telling myself I'm turning her down because I'm focusing on my goal, not because the only woman I want to be inside of is the one who's off-limits to me.

At least if I were to accept the latter, I could take some credit, unlike Persephone's bastard fiancé, who I saw going off to one of the rooms with a topless woman on each arm.

Because we all work together, I might have been able to play the naïve idiot and assume they were talking business, if I didn't see him sucking their tits.

"What about when you finish? I can wait for you. I'm sure I can show you a really good time." Seduction fills her eyes, and she runs her hands over her breasts, squeezing them so her nipples look harder.

I don't disbelieve a word she says, but my answer is still going to be no.

"Sorry, sweetheart, not tonight."

Although she looks disappointed, she still smiles. "Well, you know where to find me."

Sauntering away, she walks with a sway to her shapely hips, showing off her ass. I stare after her knowing I must have gone fucking crazy.

But I accept it.

I switch my gaze away from her when she returns to the bar and scan the room. This is one of the many function rooms at the Grand Vittorio.

The scene before me looks like a cross between a brothel and a boardroom meeting. There are topless waitresses all around and men in suits carrying flutes of champagne.

Seated around a large mahogany table in the center of the room are ten of the wealthiest men in the world playing a high-stakes poker game.

Emilio is sitting at the head with his personal waitress next to him filling his glass the instant it empties. She is completely naked and was sitting on his lap when I first arrived.

This is the other side of Emilio, the wealthy I-can-do-whatever-the-fuck-I-want side who owns people. It's not the father who asked me to protect his daughter if trouble came.

That girl on his lap has to be younger than his daughter. She couldn't be more than eighteen. Like Melissa was.

I wonder if Persephone knows what kind of man her father is.

A man of many faces who knows some of the most twisted fuckers on the planet. All those men at the table with him dabble in the sex trade and have prostitution rings in every corner of the globe.

This side of Emilio is the part I want to kill.

It's the side that would have enticed my sister into a world darker than the one she knew.

It's amazing; she grew up in the Bratva and was raised by a man who trained assassins, and not once did she ever have to worry for her life.

We took care of her.

I took care of her and promised I always would.

That's why I die just a little more every day when I wonder why she didn't come to me when she was in trouble.

She turned to drugs after the accident which killed our adopted parents. She blamed herself for their deaths because they were on the way to pick her up from the airport after a school trip.

It didn't matter what anyone told her; she still blamed herself.

I never knew this would happen. That it would get this far, where she's dead, and I'm here in the dragon's lair seeking blood.

I have answers to some of my questions, but I still don't know how it was Melissa came to be working for Emilio.

How the fuck did she even meet him, and when?

Seeing him with his waitress makes me wonder if she was just a worker, or if he ever slept with her.

Both possibilities enrage me.

I wish she'd never met him. But more than that, I wish Melissa had never met Judas.

He'd already killed her when he stabbed her in her head and her heart.

He left the knife in her stomach for a reason, though. That blow wasn't meant for her but for her baby.

She was three months pregnant and, like everything else, I didn't know.

That bastard killed her and his child in one of the worst ways possible. There is no forgiveness for that.

I tear my gaze away from the table and look around to change the view. If I'm not careful, the usual boredom will set in, and I can't allow that any more than I can allow my thoughts to drift back to Persephone.

My attention is drawn to the balcony when a man approaches the patent rail.

There's nothing special about him, but he looks shifty. He keeps my attention when he starts walking a little faster.

I keep my eyes on him, and it's not until he reaches into his pocket and I catch sight of his silver gun that I snap into action.

I move away from the corner when he aims at Emilio, pull out my gun, and shoot him before he can cock the hammer.

The sound of my gunfire and the man falling over the rail has the women screaming and the men scrambling, looking around to figure out what's going on.

I barely get the chance to do so before another gun man emerges, coming from the same place the previous one did. And he's aiming for Emilio again.

This time, I have to knock Emilio to the floor to save him. The bullet whizzes past us and lodges in the chair.

On seeing that, the shooter runs back the way he came, but more men like him burst through the door and start shooting up the place.

As the other guards shoot back, Frankie rushes to our side.

"Emilio, you okay?" he shouts.

"I'm fine," Emilio replies.

I look him over and see that, with the exception of his eyepatch falling off, the motherfucker is fine. How twisted it is that I, the man who wants to kill him, just saved his life.

What's more interesting is that I'm not the only motherfucker who wants him dead.

There seems to be a line of us waiting for a turn. Except I can't allow those behind to skip ahead because Emilio is my only link to Judas.

"You guys stay here," I say to them both.

Before either can answer, I leave them. The shooter who ran away would have only done so for a reason if the other man came in and opened fire.

He is who I'm going after.

Taking cover behind the pillars, I manage to reach the main door. When a fucker wearing a mask rushes me, I grab my knife from my back pocket and slice his throat. He's dead before he can lift a finger to attack me.

I throw the knife into the heart of another guy who comes from the left, then I rush through the door.

I follow the corridor around to the only entrance I know they could have used and kill more men as they come toward me.

I take the stairs down to the next floor, and that's when I see the door to the vault is open. The place where Emilio keeps all his secrets.

It's supposed to be sealed off, and only those above a

certain paygrade are permitted access, yet the fucking door is wide open.

The guards who are always at the door lie dead on the floor, and there are more inside, lining the path.

I follow the path and find the guy who tried to kill Emilio with two other men who are coming out of one of the storage rooms.

When they see me, both open fire.

Thinking on my feet, I take down the two with a bullet to the head when I pull my other gun, but I shoot the guy who tried to kill Emilio in the chest.

He falls to the ground like his dead friends and tries to crawl away.

In the Bratva, when you're trained to kill, you never miss a target and you never spare a life unless you want to keep them alive for a reason.

I walk up to him just as he's about to reach for a gun on the ground nearby, kick him so he flips onto his back, and step on his wound.

He screams in agonizing pain, and louder when I press the tip of my shoe into his skin.

"Who the fuck sent you?" I demand, aiming my gun at his head.

"Fuck you, dog."

I answer that remark by shooting him in his left arm. He shouts again.

"One more time. Who sent you?"

"As if I'm going to tell you."

"Okay, I'll play. I'll torture the answer out of you."

"No, you won't." He pops something in his mouth, and it's too late when I realize what it is.

It's a poisonous tablet, and there's only one group of people I know who do that.

I crouch down, and from experience, I roll up the sleeve of his shirt on his left arm and find exactly what I'm looking for. It's a tattoo of a dagger with a snake curling around the handle.

This man was not just some random hitman you hire for a kill. Of course, he wouldn't be if he hoped to kill Emilio Vittorio.

He's from a group called The Order.

Mostly, they're terrorists, and there are several factions of them who work for all sorts of people nobody wants to fuck with.

They're also the best people you hire for jobs like this —the assassination of a mafia boss.

LUKIYAN

"I want all hands on deck," Emilio demands, looking at the circle of guards who have gathered in the function room. His nostrils are flared and his eyes blazing with fury; he hasn't bothered to cover up his bad eye. "Get to the streets and find out how this happened and where they came from."

The guards rush off, but I remain behind. He looks at me as if he was expecting me to do that.

"They were from The Order," I tell him.

His jaw tenses, but he doesn't look as alarmed as I thought he would.

That, however, doesn't surprise me because I suspected he knew trouble was coming and he knew who from. Why else would he ask me to protect his daughter if something happened to him?

"I'll investigate and bear that in mind."

"You and I both know whoever hired them to kill you is hot shit. Hotter than you, obviously."

"Like I said, I'll investigate. Thank you for what you did. Now please join the others."

He's holding shit back from me. Clearly.

"It would be more helpful if I knew the rest of the story."

"Mr. Romanechka, what you need to do is your job, and that is whatever I tell you to do."

Antonio chooses that moment to walk up like the cavalry come to save the day, as if I didn't just risk my neck to save his boss and soon-to-be father-in-law.

"Come on, let me get you home," he says, flashing me a dismissive look.

I'd be lying if I didn't admit to feeling a twinge of jealousy.

Frankie comes up to me when the two walk off. "Let's go grab a drink. I'm gonna hang around for a bit to help out."

I nod and follow him to the bar. He pours us both a scotch, and we sit at the nearest table.

"Looks like I would have lost another brother if not for you," he states, taking a sip of his drink. Ice clinks against the crystal glass when he sets it down on the table and pours more scotch to replace what he drank.

"I was just doing my job."

"You moved fast, that's what I saw. That's some skill."

He's right, but that's what makes me good at what I do. "Thanks."

"I think it's only fair you're told what's going on. Emilio's been trying to keep things under wraps, but look what happened tonight."

Instantly, my interest piques. "What's going on, Frankie? They tried to kill him, and they were looking for something in the vault. That shootout in here was a distraction to kill two birds with one stone. And how the hell did they get in the vault in the first place, much less in the fucking building?"

I've searched every time I've been here, so no one can tell me that's not suspicious. Someone let them in.

He releases a slow haggard sigh. "Your job wasn't just an opening. You are a replacement for a Capo who was murdered a few weeks ago."

I didn't know that. I looked into everything I could while I was still in L.A., but if it's not recorded anywhere, there's no way of knowing.

"Murdered?"

"Yeah. It was another assassination attempt on Emilio's life. Not like this, though. Tonight was worse. The Capo's name was Patrick. He'd been with us for years, and was the kind of man who was loyal to us. He diffused the situation before it could get out of hand and was killed at the same time. He died at our warehouse. They knew Emilio was going to be there that day."

Well, hell. This is interesting. "It's quite a thing when enemies come after a man like Emilio."

"They came because they were empowered to do so

without fear of death. The last time that happened, he lost his wife and we lost our older brother."

"My condolences."

"Thank you."

"Do you have any idea why someone wants Emilio dead? Or even what they were looking for?" There was nothing in that storage cubicle in the vault.

Frankie chuckles without humor. It's a hollow sound that raises the hair on the back of my neck. "I don't know the answer either of those. Emilio is a man with many secrets and enemies. At least I know he didn't accidentally kill anyone this time."

That's what happened when Emilio's wife and brother were killed. It was a revenge killing after his actions led to the death of his enemy's son.

Frankie is, however, mistaken if he thinks Emilio didn't accidentally kill anyone because that's why I'm here.

He sets his shoulders back. "My guess is whatever they were looking for is going to be something of black market value. That's also a good reason to want him dead. So he can't retaliate."

Black market value. Fuck me.

What if it's the same thing he's working on with Judas?

"Any ideas on how men from the Order got in or *who* let them in? Because you know someone did, right?" I hate to be the new guy pointing out the obvious fact that they have a two-faced rat among them.

"No. I don't know, and that worries me because nobody gets by me. I worry something else will happen since they didn't get what they came for. I'm sure you know, bad men respect no distinction when it comes to targets. They'll kill. I don't want either of my nieces getting caught up in that. Especially Persephone. She's been through enough already."

I don't want that for her either.

"What happened last night?" Aleksei stretches one heavily-tattooed arm over his head and yawns.

"Tons of shit."

It's early—six a.m. early. Way too early for either of us to be talking business without coffee, or something stronger in my case.

After last night, I need a joint and several bottles of whiskey to numb my mind.

I joined the other guards in the investigation. We worked all night only to come up with nothing.

I knew that was going to happen though, because that's how The Order work. They leave nothing behind to trace them; that's why they kill themselves.

Aleksei and I decided to meet at a coffeehouse in the heart of Brooklyn so we could catch up properly. This was the best time to see each other without any time constraints.

The waitress comes over with our coffee, and the strong scent tickles my nose.

As soon as she sets mine down, I pick it up and take a swig. The sharpness hits my tastebuds and goes straight to my brain, giving me the wakeup I need to bring Aleksei up to speed.

Once I do, he sits back and gives me a pensive stare.

"Fuck, someone wants to kill the guy we want to kill, too," he mutters, resting his elbow on the table.

"I can't let them get to him first, Aleksei. I can't. Last night was a close call."

"I agree. So you're going to protect him?" He raises a hard brow.

This is so fucked up. "I guess so. I have to." What other choice do I have? "I can't lose this chance. It's been too long already. My sister has been dead for over six months and I haven't found her killer. So I have to do whatever it takes."

"Alright. I can look into things on my end and do what I can to find out who's behind it."

"Thanks."

I don't want to care about Emilio. I want him as dead as the fuckers who are after him. However, he's my path to Judas Kane.

That is the only thing I need to focus on.

"I'm really interested in this item they tried to take, though. If we're talking about the black market, and all of this started happening weeks ago, I think it's safe to assume this might be the same thing Judas is going to sell for Emilio."

"That's what I thought. Can we try to find out what it could be? Emilio has listed all the items kept in that vault."

"I'll take a look." He nods. "Who knows, this could help track Judas down."

"It could." Being clued in on everything helps.

"Leave it with me. Here's hoping this might give us another lead."

We can hope.

PERSEPHONE

Music fills my ears when I turn down the corridor.

Moonlight bathes my path in a silver glow.

I follow it, knowing she's in here somewhere. I just have to get to her.

Floorboards creek beneath my feet with every step I take.

I'm almost there now.

Athena will be in her room with the baby.

I continue down the silver path and go through the door ahead. There I find her, sitting by the window humming a lullaby to the tiny baby in her arms.

Athena is wearing a white dress. It's a wedding dress—my wedding dress.

She turns to look at me with her bright green eyes and smiles. Our eye color was the only difference between us.

I return the smile and move closer.

"I didn't think you'd mind me wearing this," she says in that ghostly voice I've gotten used to since she died.

"I don't."

"She's sleeping now." She lays the baby back in the crib.

I look at Lilah's little hands balled into tiny fists as she settles into sleep. She looks just like when she was alive, too.

When I return my focus to Athena, she's already looking at me.

She presses a dainty finger to my chest and traces a line down my scar.

"It's fragile. Don't let them break your heart."

"Yours," I mumble.

"No, yours now." I look down at my chest as blood pours from my heart.

Blood, thick and dark, flows from the scar and starts gushing out of my body, covering her and the baby.

"Goodbye, Persephone."

Her face turns into a skeleton, and maggots cover her body.

I scream.

The terror rips me out of the nightmare, and I'm gasping so hard I can't catch my breath.

When I manage to, I realize I'm covered in a cold sweat, but my mind is so disorientated I can't even remember falling asleep, or which is the dream world and what is reality.

Feeling my scar, I quickly confirm the truth. If I'm here, it means she's not.

Everything that happened really did happen.

Mom died.

Lilah died.

Athena died.

It's just me and Father left.

It's hard to believe our happy little family was ripped apart in such a cruel, punishing way.

And by a man we trusted with all our hearts. It was one of the guards who let the enemy in. They planned it, and wanted us all dead.

Chills cascade down my spine when I realize where I am, and my back goes ramrod straight.

I'm in her room again—in Athena's room. And in my lap is one of Lilah's little dresses.

I pick it up and look at it and my surroundings.

Once again I have no memory of coming in here, much less falling asleep.

This isn't the first time this has happened to me. It just hasn't happened in a while. Until today I would have thought I was cured, but I can't be because I still have her heart—a piece of her still lives inside me, fueling my borrowed life.

The life I borrowed from her.

When Athena first died, I used to have these strange dreams. Only I'm not sure if they were dreams.

They were always of me either tending to the baby or painting.

When I woke up, I'd find myself in here or in the room that used to be the nursery. On many occasions, Father would find me mindlessly trying to finish off one of Athena's paintings, or folding baby clothes.

It's as if more than just my sister's heart lives on in me.

It's like I have her memories. Or... maybe it's more like her regrets.

Regrets of all the things she never got to do, like be a mother to the little girl she loved with all her heart and lost.

I'm not sure which drove her crazy; losing a child, or getting pregnant the way she did.

No... I can't think about that.

I mustn't. If I do, I'll hate myself even more.

I snap my eyes shut as the truth works its way into my mind, and I shake it free.

We don't talk about the truth enough because it hurts worse than the lies we live by to get from one day to the next.

That's why the silence worked its way in and opened the door to madness.

We did that to ourselves.

Madness touched me too, because it's only when I'm stressed out that I have these weird experiences I can't explain.

It feels like I'm always dancing on the edge of limbo, neither living nor dead but permanently stuck between the world of the living and that of the dead.

I didn't like the way Father and I left things yesterday.

All our talk confirmed was that I was right about the way he feels toward me.

And there's nothing I can do about it. No fucking wonder I found myself here.

Now I just have to suck it up and move on. Easier said than done.

The door opens at the same time I stand, making me jump.

It's Raven.

Judging from the way she's panting I can tell she must have been running.

"I heard screaming." She looks me up and down and takes note of the little dress in my hands. "Are you okay?"

"I'm fine. I had a nightmare."

"I'm not surprised." She comes in closing the door behind her. "Persephone, what are you doing in here? You shouldn't be here, and with that." She points to the little dress.

I bring it to my chest the way Athena used to after Lilah died.

To me the dress still smells of new baby. I can still see her wearing it with her vibrant toothless smile, and feel her in my arms.

"I'm okay." I dare not tell her what happened. I don't want to spend my last two days here with people thinking I'm crazy.

"I don't know why your father doesn't do something different with this room. It's not healthy to keep it this way." She shakes her head with sadness.

I understand perfectly what she means. Athena's room is the same as it has always been. All her books are on the shelf just the way she left them, her clothes in the wardrobe, and her bed neatly made. It's as if she's going to come back any moment.

"He can't let them go. It's his way of dealing with the loss." Although we don't see eye to eye, I understand my father.

"Come here." She steps forward and hugs me.

I hug her back harder. "Thanks, I think I needed that."

When she pulls away, she takes the dress from me. "Persephone, it really isn't healthy for you to be in here. I know how you feel when it comes to Athena. I don't want you feeling worse."

"I know. I guess I just miss her like crazy." I press my lips together.

"That's completely understandable. I miss her too. We all do. But, Persephone… you know she did what she did out of love. Right?"

I nod slowly. "Yeah. I know. I do know." It doesn't make knowing what she did for me any easier. But I know her sacrifice was for me.

"I, um, hate to be the bearer of bad news," she begins with a tentative expression. "Especially when you look like you could use a break."

"What's happened now?"

"Antonio is here."

My temper immediately flares. What the hell does he want?

I wasn't expecting him.

"Why is he here?"

She raises her shoulders. "You know him. He just said

he wanted to see you. I actually came by to take you to lunch."

Lunch? Is it that late?

"What time is it?"

"It's nearly one in the afternoon."

Oh my God. I can't remember when I last slept that late. It's the exhaustion from the crazy week and the fact that most nights see me either not sleeping at all or having only a few meager hours of broken sleep.

"I really don't want to deal with him right now."

"I'm sorry. He's waiting for you in your living room."

That asshole. He knows how I feel about him entering my space, but of course, since I'm a thing that must do as she's told, my opinion doesn't matter.

Dragging in a breath, I summon courage. "It's okay. I'll be okay."

I just have to grin and bear the shit for today and tomorrow.

Tomorrow night, I'll be gone from this hell.

"You know how I hate to be kept waiting," Antonio says when I walk into my living room.

He's sitting on my little beige sofa, looking out of place next to the painting Athena did of a ballet dancer on the wall behind.

He doesn't fit anywhere in my life, so everything about him feels out of place.

It's ironic, seeing him in here feels creepier than when I found Lukiyan in my bedroom.

"I wasn't expecting you. Do we have a meeting?" Best to be professional. It's the easiest way to maneuver him.

"Come here." He stands and glares at me.

Biting down hard on my back teeth, I walk closer to him and stop a good length away so if he comes at me, I can still run through the door.

"Where is your ring?" He glances at my hand that should be wearing my engagement ring.

"It's in my room. I must have forgotten to but it back on after my shower last night. What do you want, Antonio?" Best to dance around the subject and skip to something else.

"You know what I want." Dark seduction flashes in his eyes, and bile rises up my throat. "I want to fuck you. Now take off your clothes and get on your hands and knees."

My heartbeat speeds up, galloping a million miles an hour as I think of all the things I could do to get out of this situation I've feared for months.

My grin-and-bear-it tactic only marginally works. Even with that, I've been lucky to get away with just giving him a blow job.

"Did you hear me?"

"I heard you, but I'm not doing it," I snap. Fuck it. I can't let him fuck me.

I just can't. I can't bear the thought of him being inside me, much less it actually happening.

"Are you telling me no?" He steps forward.

I back away, but he grabs my arm, digging his fingers into my skin.

"You're hurting me. Let me go."

"You deserve to be hurt, you little whore. Don't think I haven't seen the way you look at the new guard. Are you fucking him?"

"Fuck you, you fucking asshole."

I always knew I was going to snap at some point. I just didn't know when.

I also knew that when I did, I should expect him to unleash.

So when the back of his hand lands across my face, I preempted it.

Although I saw it coming and landed myself right in the heart of the shit, it doesn't make the pain hurt any less.

He hits me so hard I scream and fall to the floor. Blood runs down my mouth from my nose, and my face feels like it's going to explode.

My face, however, is the least of my worries as he rips my little camisole top right off my body, exposing my breasts.

"I'll show you who I truly am. When I'm driving into your pussy, then you'll know me." He gets on top of me and holds me down.

"Please don't. Stop, Antonio." I'm screaming the words and trying to fight him off, but he's not listening. "Please don't do this!"

He slaps me again and my stomach lurches.

My panties are ripped off me and he swoops down to crush his lips to mine, kissing me hard.

Tears pour out of my eyes, and I barely register that this is our first kiss.

When he's done plunging his tongue into my mouth, he covers it with his large, calloused hand and starts undoing his belt buckle.

I beat my fists on the floor, screaming into his hand, but it's fruitless.

He doesn't stop.

Antonio is just about to shove his pants down his legs when he's suddenly yanked backwards, right off me.

A ferocious growl fills the room, and Lukiyan comes into my view as he throws a fist in Antonio's face.

I grab my clothes so I can cover myself, but I'm shaking so much I can barely get my hands to work.

"Motherfucker, how dare you touch her!" Lukiyan shouts, throwing more punches in Antonio's face.

"She's mine. How fucking dare you come in here and interrupt us?"

Even when he's being battered, Antonio is still trying to have the upper hand. But Lukiyan takes him down several notches with his continued jabs.

Antonio manages to get a punch in when Lukiyan moves, but it's only momentarily.

Lukiyan grabs his neck, and I don't know how he's able to get him off the ground and shove him into the wall, but he does.

He pulls a knife from his back pocket, and I see the disaster that's about to happen.

Lukiyan is going to kill Antonio.

Lukiyan slices Antonio's cheek and hoists the knife to stab him in his neck, but Frankie stops it from happening when he rushes in from nowhere and grabs his arm.

"Stop. Fucking stop it!" Frankie shouts. It looks like he's using all his strength to hold Lukiyan back.

"You think beating women makes you a man?" Lukiyan wails. Although he's restrained, he still knees Antonio in his balls.

He doubles over, but Lukiyan still has a grip on him with his other hand.

"Lukiyan, fucking cut it out now and let him go." Frankie pulls Lukiyan away from Antonio and only releases him when he seems sure he won't retaliate.

Antonio is coughing up blood and his face is a mess.

Good.

He got a taste of his own medicine.

"She's not yours. Fucking asshole, look at her face." Lukiyan points at me. "If you fucking touch her again, I'll kill you."

He switches his gaze to me.

I'm still shaking and crying, but I can see that murderous look in his eyes quite clearly. The look is accompanied with those words he said to me.

I am your Hades.

He doesn't have to say them; I can hear them. I never stopped hearing them.

Now they have meaning.

I am your Hades.

I feel like his Persephone as he scans my face, looking at what I know are bad bruises.

"Take a walk, Lukiyan, and calm the fuck down," Frankie orders.

He gives Frankie a narrowed look then walks away.

I stare after him until he walks through the door and I can't see him anymore.

He saved me. He saved me again in a way I can't describe.

I'm snapped back out of my daze when Frankie rushes toward Antonio and throws a fist in his face just as he was straightening up.

"Get the fuck out of here. Get out." Frankie grabs Antonio's shoulder and shoves him forward.

When he staggers out the door, Frankie moves toward me.

"Persephone, are you okay?"

I shake my head and hold my clothes closer to my naked form.

He grabs one of my throws from the sofa and wraps it around me, then he holds me as I break down, crying from deep, deep, deep within.

For everything.

PERSEPHONE

I waited for night to fall before I decided to come out here.

I'm at the cottage by the lake where Lukiyan is staying.

Maybe coming out here to see him is a bad idea, but I wanted to talk to him properly before I disappear.

I wanted to thank him for what he did today.

Inside, the cottage is dark and there's no sign of life, so I'm hoping he's here.

This will probably be the only chance I get to see him without everyone around.

I'm sure he'll be at the fundraiser tomorrow, but it will be too late then.

The cool night air stings my skin where it's bruised as I walk through the rose garden and head to the door. The entire left side of my face was so swollen earlier that I looked like a football. The swelling has gone down now, thanks to Frankie, but the bruises are there and even when they're gone, I know I'll still feel them.

Before I knock on the door, the splash of water catches my attention. It's not in the lake, so it must be coming from the pool at the back of the house.

I make my way around there and stop by the archway when I see Lukiyan doing laps in the pool.

The amber light from the solar panels shines down on him, highlighting his athletic ability to glide through the water and own it the way he does everything else.

I'm hidden in the shadow of the archway so he can't see me, but that doesn't mean he doesn't know I'm here.

I get the feeling he does.

Powerful arms lined with muscle and tattoos slice through the water. Then he stops at the other end of the pool and gets out, revealing he's naked.

My entire body melts from the heat that instantly consumes me as I watch him, taking in every inch of his perfection. Rock-hard muscles flex when he bends down to grab a towel.

Instead of wrapping it around himself, he dries his hair and turns to face me, showing his erect cock, long and massive, bobbing before him.

Christ.

It doesn't matter where I am, asleep or awake, I lose myself when I'm around this man. I become instantly aroused, and it feels raw and primal.

As if I ever stood a chance of resisting the temptation that draws me to him.

"You can come out now, unless you want to stay there all night," he says.

I was obviously right that he knew I was here.

When I step out of the shadows, he does nothing to cover his cock.

He continues drying his body, and hair, but purposely leaves his cock exposed.

I'm grateful for the partial darkness to hide the wild blush sweeping over my pale skin.

"Is this what you do in your spare time? Swim naked and rescue damsels in distress?"

He continues to stare at me, but his expression lacks emotion.

"It looks that way."

"I'm not sure if those are things Hades would do."

"Well, he did them today." He covers himself now, wrapping the towel around his waist. "How's your face?"

"It's seen better days. Thank you for what you did for me."

"You don't have to thank me for that." He sighs and tenses the square line of his jaw. "You shouldn't be here, Persephone."

My lips part to answer but he walks into the house, leaving me.

I'd dismiss myself if I knew tomorrow wouldn't change everything for me, so I follow him in.

It's been a while since I came here. The guards have always lived here.

This was where Patrick, the Capo who died, used to

live. Although he worked for my father for years, I never really spoke to him. He was one of the silent types.

Lukiyan walks into the kitchen and grabs himself a beer out of the fridge.

He sets it on the countertop and gets out some orange juice and a glass from the cabinet. He pours some and hands it to me.

I'm not thirsty, but I take it, and he watches me down the contents.

"Why shouldn't I be here? I had to say thanks."

"You just shouldn't be."

"Well, I am. God knows what would have happened to me if you hadn't come along." I know he's going to get in trouble for what he did, if he hasn't already. "I am grateful."

"You're welcome."

I study his face, and the myriad of questions I had about him rush back to me.

"All I know is your name."

"My name?"

"Yeah, and I suppose since you spoke Russian to me the other night and your surname sounds like it, I guessed you must be that nationality. Are you?"

He stares at me for a moment before he straightens.

"I'm half Russian."

"Which half?"

"My mother."

"Did you ever live in Russia?"

"I was born there, but I grew up here in the States."

"That's cool. I was born in Brazil. I'm sure you know this already, but I have family there. That's why I was there and how we met. How come you were there?"

"I needed a break."

"What from?"

"No…"

His answer stuns me. "No to what?"

"This isn't twenty questions. You still don't get to know about me."

"Why?"

He takes a swig of his beer and presses his lips together. "Because it's best."

"How about three questions, then?"

He smirks and considers the request for a moment. A bubble of excitement fills me when he nods. "Okay, three questions. You don't give up, do you?"

"No, not so much."

"I didn't think so. You get three questions, but I don't have to give you an answer to any."

I chuckle, and his gaze drops to my lips. "How is that fair?"

"Take it or leave it."

"I'll take it."

"I get three questions, too, and you *have* to answer those."

Well played. I wish I'd thought of that. This could be a bad idea, but my curiosity about him is getting the better of me.

"You got it. Me first, though."

"Alright. Go for it, but choose wisely."

I want to ask about where he came from but decide against it. I have better questions for him. More meaningful questions that I hope he'll answer.

I think of the first one. It's an easy one he should answer.

"How old are you?" I ask.

"Twenty-eight."

Although he acts older, I could have guessed he was in his twenties from his cool style and the youthfulness in his face.

"You act older."

"I have to. My turn," he says. "When did you start dancing?"

That's a question I love, and I can't help but smile. "My mother told me I've been dancing since I first learned to walk. I heard the music and fell in love with it. I never looked back."

When I get to where I'm going, I'll give it a little while until things settle before I plan to find some way of dancing. I figured it's not going to be too hard to find somewhere like that in Europe.

"I could tell. Your turn again."

This next question is one I've mulled over for months. So, I don't have to think about it at all.

"Back in Brazil, what made you choose me?" It was odd, at least I thought so.

I was dancing by myself at the club and now that I

think of it, I must have looked like a loner. I was clearly there by myself.

The only men I think would have picked me up were the ones with bad intentions. But this one just wanted a night with me.

He steps closer, reaches out to take a lock of my hair, and I'm reminded of us that night again.

"You're beautiful." He speaks in a low, almost reverent voice that gives me goosebumps. Not because he's scared me, but more so because I've never had anyone look at me the way he is, or sound the way he sounds in relation to me.

It's like he sees me as something hallowed.

"You think I'm beautiful?"

"Is that another question?"

"No. You can elaborate, can't you?"

He inches closer and the raw, masculine scent of him fills me with need and carnal desire.

"Persephone, goddess of spring and things that live and flourish in beauty. Yes, I think you're beautiful." He holds my gaze, his eyes piercing my soul, peering into my mind to seek my inner thoughts. I always try to mask everything—the good and the bad—but I don't want to with him. "My turn."

"Your turn."

He plants one thick finger on my chest and smooths away the fabric of my top so he can see the tattoo covering my scar.

I know what he's looking at, and I know what he'll ask

even before he opens his mouth. I just don't know if I can hold up my end of the deal and give him an answer.

"What happened to you here? That's not just a tattoo." There it is.

I feel like I should have known he would ask me that question.

I continue to stare at him, trying to formulate an answer that doesn't hurt, except I can't think of one.

Since I try to never think about the fine print of why I'm still alive and my twin isn't, it's hard to come up with an answer.

"Surgery."

Worry clouds his eyes, and I relish in it. Seeing his emotion for me clings to my mind in a way I can't describe.

"What kind of surgery?"

"Is that your third question?" I try to play smart.

"You know it's not. We can elaborate, can't we?" He borrows my words, and I don't blame him.

"Yes, we can."

"What kind of surgery did you have?"

"Heart surgery." Tears prick the backs of my eyes as I push away the rest of that truth. I don't have to tell him any more than I already have.

I've never had to talk about it because everyone knew what happened. When I disappear, I'll never have to talk about it with anyone again, and I'll never have my father's judging eyes on me, making me feel like I don't deserve life.

"Are you okay now?"

I nod, then he surprises me by lowering his head to plant a kiss on the base of my scar. He then proceeds to drop one kiss after another up the line of butterflies and roses forming my tattoo, his lips leaving fire in their wake as he makes his way up.

It's the sexiest thing I've ever had done to me.

My God. My body comes alive with wild energy, and I want him to do so much more to me.

He soothes the ache in my soul and arouses me at the same time because it's unbecoming of him.

I'm not ready for him to pull away. I don't want him to.

"Your turn," he rasps.

I have to take a quick gulp of air to clear my mind. I had the questions all there, but they've faded.

Think, Persephone, get yourself together. You can't be this aroused every time you see this man.

But I am, and he knows it. The wicked smirk on his ridiculously handsome face tells me he knows exactly what he's doing to me. It has to be sinful to be so gorgeous and sexy at the same time.

What's my question?

"What made you work for my father?" I ask him that because I'll always wonder how it was he came back to me.

"It's a good job, and he pays well." The answer feels like a lie and the truth rolled into one, which can't be good.

I know working for my father is exactly what he says,

but part of me doesn't believe that's why he'd want the job.

"That was your last question, Persephone. My turn."

"Go for it."

I don't know what else he might ask me, but there's a lot I don't want to answer.

"Why'd you give your virginity to me?"

Like that. I think for a moment and decide to go with the truth because I think he'll understand.

"I didn't want the monster to have it. I wanted to choose. That day, my birthday, my father signed me away to Antonio. I never saw it coming even though I knew he was going to marry me off. I just never expected it would be to that bastard. I hate him." I hate Antonio even more for what he did to me earlier.

So tomorrow has to work. I can't fail and be left here to live a life with a man who will end me.

Lukiyan leans forward again and I lift my head.

He looms before me and presses a finger to my lips, tracing the outline of my mouth.

"He doesn't deserve you. No one does, not even me."

"But I gave myself to you." I don't know why I said that. It's meaningless and will never have any bearing.

Nevertheless, it's the truth.

He presses his finger into my jaw, coming closer so he's a kiss away.

"I still didn't deserve you."

"You're my Hades."

Something flashes in his eyes as the words fall from

my lips. He stares back at me with an open expression, as if the walls he's built up have crumbled away.

There's a moment of silence that seems to stretch for eons, and I don't know what he'll do next.

The silence becomes thick, like tar, and just as daunting.

Then he closes the space between us when he moves to my lips and gives me another forbidden kiss. It's a mere brush over my mouth that feels too chaste for him, almost like he's tasting me.

Once he gets the taste and I do, too, we both kiss each other harder, as if we should have always been kissing and never apart.

His tongue swoops into my mouth and dances with mine in the most delicious way, luring me to the dark side.

He pulls away and moves down to my breast, sucking my left nipple through the fabric of my tank top before he moves it away completely along with the cup of my bra, exposing the pleading nipple so he can suck it properly.

Arousal claws within me as the hot pleasure courses through my veins like lava in a volcano ready to erupt.

The ounce of awareness that's left in my mind cautions that we're right by the kitchen window. Anyone passing by would be able to see us. And it could be anyone.

Father, Antonio, Raven, or one of the other guards.

But I don't care. I'm so sick of having to tiptoe around what I want to do, and I'm sick of worrying.

Fuck everything and everyone. If Lukiyan is going to fuck me right here against the wall, it's happening.

He pulls my other breast out, and sucks on it, giving my body the attention it craves.

Madness consumes me when he slips his hand under my skirt to cup my sex and starts massaging my pussy.

His fingers slide into my panties, and he rubs my already swollen clit.

"You're so wet. Always wet for me. Do you want me to fuck you, Persephone?"

It must be a rhetorical question because my body is begging to be fucked.

"Yes."

He returns to my lips and gives me a cruel, punishing kiss that leaves me breathless. Keeping his hands on my pussy he plunges his finger in and out of my wet passage. First it's hard, like he's fucking me, then slow and caressing.

I can feel his hard cock pressing into my belly through the towel, and I want to touch it. So I do. I rub along his length and try to get to it through the towel.

When Lukiyan pulls out of the kiss, I think he's going to continue what he's doing to me, but he doesn't, and when he takes my hand off his cock and I see the guarded look return to his eyes, my hopes crash.

He catches my face and gives me a long, hard stare. He almost seems like a different person from the version he was only moments ago.

"Sweet Persephone, I've never met another woman

who was more greedy for my dick. But I'm not going to make you my whore tonight."

He is different. His choice of words feel like they were selected to hurt me and bring me down from the wild sexual high he took me to.

And they do.

"I'm not a whore."

"You are when you're with me. But you don't belong to me. You're his."

Antonio's.

"You said I wasn't."

He gives me a flinty gaze. "It doesn't matter what I say. You belong to him. Now go home. I'm not going to give you what you came for."

I pull out of his grasp, covering myself as humiliation consumes me.

"I came to thank you."

"That was just an excuse to get fucked."

"Why are you such an asshole?" I swallow hard.

"Go home."

Everyone talks to me like I'm a child. I never expected him to do it, too.

But it's worse with him because he rejected me.

"Goodbye, Hades." I mean that as my final thought for this nonsense.

Turning on my heels, I leave, never looking back.

Goodbye forever, Lukiyan. I wish I'd never met you.

I'm in enough pain as it is, but he's the only person who's ever made me feel broken.

LUKIYAN

"You know why you're here, don't you?" Emilio states. I hold my breath, hoping like fuck I didn't fuck myself over.

"I do."

"Good." He stares me down like a man who wants to kill.

I understand that thirst all too well. I feel it now as I stare back at him from across the table.

We're in a different office. This one is at the Valencia, the second biggest hotel in his chain. It's named after his first wife, Persephone's mother.

The fundraiser has already begun. Just like I anticipated, he wanted to see me first. This wouldn't have been Frankie's doing. It's Antonio's.

"I'm just going to cut to the chase," he adds, squaring his shoulders. "You're only still here because you're useful to me, and that's why I'm keeping you. Do what you did yesterday again, and not only are you gone, but I will make sure you never work for anybody ever again. Understand?"

"I understand." And I'm relieved, but I don't feel any better.

I feel just as much of an asshole as I did when I rejected Persephone last night.

I wanted her so badly but I stopped myself from taking her, because of this.

I can't lose myself the way I do when I'm with her and fuck things up to get Judas. Thinking with my dick is going to make me lose everything.

I know beating up Antonio crossed the line just as much as what I did with Persephone mere hours later.

It's their custom for a man to own a woman and punish her as he sees fit once she's signed over to him. I just couldn't stand by and allow him to rape her.

Her pleas for him to stop reminded me of my birth mother's. When her boyfriends used to batter her, they'd batter me, too, because I was always trying to help. I helped until she wouldn't let me, and I guess that last time would have been my final moment, too. I'd be as dead now as she is.

"He was going to rape her," I add, because I think he should know. "You asked me to take care of your daughter, but you signed her over to a man who would beat her. I don't get it."

His nostrils flare. "I am the leader here. You don't get to take matters into your own hands with a man I've chosen to marry my daughter to. Don't think I'm blind to the way you look at her. I know your intentions aren't *just* to protect her."

He's not wrong, but he's still a dick.

"I don't think you're blind, sir. But with every due respect, when you think of it, I was doing what you asked me to do."

"Get out before I change my mind."

I get up and make my way out of the office. I walk down the corridor and head out to the terrace, where I'm met with the cool air and the salty scent of the sea.

We're right by the docks. Rows of ships, big and small, line the marina, and their lights look like a nest of twinkling stars.

I don't want to be here, and I'm sick of this waiting game.

My phone rings in my back pocket and I reach for it. That's going to be Aleksei. Only he and Lucca have this number.

I already spoke to Lucca today, so I don't expect another call until next week.

When I see it's Aleksei, my hopes rise that he might have news for me.

"Hey." I press the phone to my ear.

"I found something in relation to what those guys could have been looking for. It's not much, but I think it's something we can work with."

"What did you find?"

"First I tried to check out what was in the vault. It seems that something was moved earlier that day from the section you found the men in. The thing is classified though and only goes by a number in the system. So I checked with one of my street guys back in L.A. and he said there was a piece of tech the Camorra were creating to sell on the black market. He didn't know specifically what it was, but he heard it was worth billions. That sounds like our thing."

"It does. Those guys are all about new-age tech worth a fuck load of money, and anything that could get them ahead of the game." I mull over what it could be. "Did he say anything else?"

"No. But at least we have something more definitive to look out for."

"Yes." That is something.

"Everything else okay on your end?"

"It's as good as it can be." I won't tell him how I almost jeopardized this mission.

"Alright, catch you later."

I put my phone back in my pocket when he hangs up.

Pulling in a deep breath, I will myself to focus. If only I could get the image of that disappointment I saw on Persephone's face out of my head.

My mean-spirited taunts were the real me, but I didn't mean it.

Everything else I said to her prior to that was completely outside my character.

I don't talk about gods and goddesses, or spring time and life and shit.

I did it though, because I knew she appreciated it, and

when she called me Hades, I almost believed I was him again. Until I realized the time for games is over.

Life is a deadly game, and that night we met was one of those curveballs the Universe throws at you that you can't explain.

We were supposed to be two passing ships on an unforgettable night...

Nothing more.

I turn away and head back inside the function room. My shift's about to start, and more people will be arriving.

I assume my post at the center of the second-floor balcony, where I can see everyone on the ground floor.

Across from me is Timothy, one of the other guards. He's been the most talkative of everyone, but I think it's because we're close in age. He dips his head for a curt nod and I do the same.

Boredom sets in quickly, until I see Persephone walk in through the sliding glass doors.

Dressed in a long golden gown that wraps around her decadent body, Persephone Vittorio commands attention with her beauty and poise like the goddess she is.

As she graces the world with her presence, I'm reminded of the inadequate word I used to describe her yesterday. I called her beautiful, but it wasn't enough.

Her hair is piled on top of her head in a sexy bun of curls clustered together, which carries off the look and accentuates her long, elegant neck.

There isn't a man here who isn't staring at her. From

the corner of the room, Antonio strides across to her and takes her arm.

I want to chop that arm off just for touching her.

She's not his. She's not mine either, but I want her to be.

Watching her with him—the monster—feels like a punishment, even if she looks like she doesn't want to be with him.

I hate it, and I hate that I have to tamp down my rage so I don't give myself away and fuck myself over even more than I already have.

I continue to stare at her. She must feel the intensity of my gaze because she looks right up at me, and our eyes lock for a secret moment of passion before she looks away.

It feels like I've lost her for good.

Antonio holds on to her like he's afraid someone might snatch her away, and she's pressed up against him as if she's a part of his clothing.

I'm forced to watch them together for a full two hours until the speeches are made and she moves over to the table with the canapes.

She talks to Raven for a while before a man walks up to her and all he does is nod.

It's weird and piques my interest.

Then, while everyone is busy listening to the speeches, she backs out the door. I guess she's going to the ladies' room, but something pulls on my insides when half an hour passes and she doesn't return.

I decide to go down and see what's happening.

I check the ladies' first and don't find her. Then I look into several other rooms and still find no trace of her.

Panic sets in, and I decide to head down the fire escape because it's the only other place to check.

Mentally, I kick myself for waiting so long to follow her. What if something happened to her? What if one of those men snuck in and took her?

There's a fucking rat among us. What if he got to her?

Fuck. Fucking fuck.

What would I do if something happened to her?

I end up outside on the boardwalk, frantically looking around for her.

Following the path down to the pier, I continue my search. Then I catch a glimpse of long flowing hair illuminated by the moon on one of the cargo ships ahead of me.

That's her.

It's only because I have a good eye for details that I spot her and *know* it's her, even though she's now dressed in black.

She's in the boarding entrance of the ship trying to blend in with the shadows as she speaks to one of the ship's mates. A duffle bag is slung over her shoulders, and she doesn't look like she's in trouble.

It takes a nanosecond for me to realize what she's doing, but I can't believe she has the balls to do it.

She's escaping. All of this was planned.

Persephone planned it.

She raises the hood on the cape she's wearing and moves further into the ship.

When I can't see her anymore, something pinches my heart and tells me to let her go.

Let her leave so she can't marry that bastard. Better she belongs to no one than to him.

However, when I start running, I realize I can't let her go.

I'm a selfish bastard who wants her, but the other reason I can't allow her to leave is that she'll be in danger out in the world just for being Emilio Vittorio's daughter.

No matter where she's going or what plans she has, danger will find her at some point in her life, and I can't stand not being there to protect her.

Monsters like me creep around the corners lying in wait to devour.

Monsters like me take and take and take. We're selfish that way because we weren't born monsters.

We were made.

We know when to let go and when to keep holding on to something we want.

So I run with everything inside me before that ship sets sail.

I reach the ship and rush on deck with my gun held high, silencing anyone who dares to challenge me with one look.

She turns to see me, and shock registers on her pretty face.

Then she runs.

16

PERSEPHONE

No, no, no.

No, God, no. This can't be happening.

I didn't get this far only to get caught.

I run as fast as I can, but a quick look behind me confirms my fear that Lukiyan is faster and he's going to catch me.

I know it like I know my own name, but I still keep running down the ship's corridor, hoping and praying I can escape him.

I don't even know where I'm going. I just know I can't go back.

Not back to the prison that awaits me with Antonio, and Father, who hates me.

I have to keep moving forward.

Tonight was planned so carefully, and Maya did so much for me. She risked her neck and everything to help me. I can't give up.

"Persephone, stop!" His voice carries down the corridor, sounding all around me, inside and out. Then his powerful arms wrap around my middle, catching me mid-flight.

"Let go of me. Fucking let me go!" I cry. "Let me go."

"What the fuck do you think you're doing?"

"Let me go, Lukiyan."

"No. Of course I'm not fucking letting you go."

"Please, please let me go." I've resorted to begging, hoping against hope that he still might let me go because he must know what's happening here and why.

My pleas, however, fall on deaf ears because all he does is flip me over his shoulder as if I'm weightless and carries me off the ship that was supposed to sail me to freedom.

As if things aren't bad enough, the sky cracks open and rain pours down on us. That doesn't stop me from beating my fists against his back and flapping my legs.

"Fucking stop it, or I'll hand-deliver you to your father just like this."

The threat makes me freeze, and I think of the host of problems I now have. I tried to escape and Lukiyan caught me. Why would he understand what I tried to do and help me when he works for my father? I'm just a piece of ass to him, and he doesn't answer to me.

He's barely a week into a *good* job that *pays well*. So of course he's not going to help me because his allegiance is to my father.

I break all over again and crumple against his shoulder.

I'm carried to a black Merc, where he sets me in the back with my duffle bag and gets in the front with a heavy scowl on his face.

"Sit tight and be fucking quiet," he orders.

I flinch, succumbing to the misery that awaits me.

Half an hour later, we pull up at the house I never thought I was going to see again, and he escorts me to my room.

I'd made the bed earlier and packed my things away in the wardrobe, half hoping Father would leave it like he did with Athena's room.

Now I'm back, and no one knows yet that I tried to escape.

I almost did it. I would have until this bastard caught me.

"Sit down." He points to the bed.

"No, you bastard. You know what they're going to do to me."

"That is not my fucking concern. I'm just doing my job."

I don't know where the bravery comes from, but I lift my hand and slap him across his face.

I'm sick of feeling used and abused, and I can't take it from him.

My action, however, was a big mistake.

He grabs me, moves to the bed, and flips me over his knee like I'm a petulant child. Then he lands a heavy hand on my ass.

I cry out from the shock and the pain, which gets

worse when he pulls my pants down and spanks my bare ass.

"You don't fucking know what you're doing," he shouts.

Slap, slap, slap.

Tears run down my cheeks, and I wish he would stop.

"You're hurting me."

"What do you think would happen to you if the wrong kind of people got to you and decided to make an example of you?" Two more slaps are delivered to my ass, which now stings like hell. "You're Persephone Vittorio. The wrong kind of person would figure out who you are and kill you."

Another slap, and I scream, but then I feel his cock pushing into my belly and I realized the asshole is getting off on this.

And... fuck me, knowing he's aroused is making me wet.

One more slap, and the sound that comes out of me is an unmistakable moan.

On hearing it, he rests his hand gently on my ass and strokes the burning there. It's only for a moment, though, but it's effective and a juxtaposition to the cruelty he just showed me. The next second sees him breaking the brief spell and lifting me off his lap.

Quickly, I fix my clothes, then my eyes drop to the noticeable bulge pressing against his pants, and I flick my gaze up to his intense eyes as he glares at me.

"Where the hell were you going?" He balls his hands into tight fists.

"Fuck you. The time for questions is over. You had your chance to get to know me, and you didn't take it."

"Oh, yeah?"

"Yes."

"Alright, I'll bear that in mind." He turns and heads to the door.

Panic assails me and I rush after him, catching his arm before he can leave.

"Please don't tell my father. Please. I'll be locked away until the wedding." My soul aches just for hearing that word—*wedding*—come out of my mouth.

"What you did was dangerous."

"I can't marry Antonio, Lukiyan." The bravado I showed him seconds ago fades and I fall apart. "I can't do it. He'll destroy me. You know that. Look what happened yesterday. Look how he beat me. He threatened to break my legs so I'd never dance again. I can't marry him. That's why I did what I did."

Understanding forms in his eyes. Again, I think he might be seeing things my way, but I'm mistaken when he pulls his arm away from me.

"Get changed and go to bed. Don't have any more smart ideas. I'm going to watch you until your father gets back."

God, this is a nightmare.

I stare back at him in dismay as he turns away and walks out the door.

Hours have passed and nothing has happened.

I cleaned up and changed into a pair of yoga pants and a tank top. It was the first thing I could find. I knew I wasn't going to be able to sleep, so I didn't bother putting on any nightclothes.

Lukiyan hasn't been back to see me, and since I'm on this side of the house, I can never tell when people arrive on the property.

Father could be here now, getting the 411 on my latest activities, and I'll be none the wiser until he summons me to his office.

All I'm concerned with now is that I don't get Maya in trouble. We planned my escape to happen during this fundraiser because it would look like I just escaped on a boat.

When Lukiyan tells Father what really happened, he'll know someone helped me.

Lukiyan also has my duffle bag with all the documents. Fake ID's and a fake passport scream of someone helping me.

So, I don't know how I'm even going to start explaining that. Not to mention that trying to escape a marriage contract is the same as high treason. They might not kill me, but the punishment will be comparable to death.

I'm going crazy just waiting here.

It's after midnight already, so I'm not sure what's happening.

Maybe Lukiyan decided to go to bed. Maybe Father isn't even here and he decided to stay at the hotel with Alecia, or someone else.

I remember when they first got married, she tried to get rid of my mother's things, and Father lost his shit.

Alecia didn't just want to be the replacement; she wanted to be the one. The woman Father loved more than Mom.

Even if I didn't know he doesn't love her, I knew he would never love her as much as my mother.

I have my own trouble, but the thought of Father cheating on Alecia's pompous ass makes me smile to myself. If I'm smiling with the situation I'm in, it must mean I've finally lost my mind.

It's just that I know she'll take pleasure in my demise when I get punished.

What is going on, though?

I have to find out.

I slip off the bed and make my way out of my room into the dark corridor. The lights don't pop on like they usually do, but I have the moonlight to guide me.

I proceed down the long winding corridor, looking for Lukiyan, feeling silly with every step I take.

Clearly, he's gone back to the cottage.

But what if he hasn't? I need to check and be sure.

I head down the first set of stairs, and as I turn onto

the next corridor, the faint sound of his deep baritone washes over me.

He's talking to someone.

Is it Father?

If it is, then I am very foolish indeed, and all I'm doing is accelerating the time to receive my punishment.

Lukiyan continues talking, but whoever he's talking to doesn't answer, which makes me believe he's on the phone.

It sounds like he could be in the hall where the sculptures are, so I head there.

Stealthily, I take my steps lightly, slipping through the door, which is a jar.

He's at the end of the hall, near the Rococo curtains. He has the phone pressed against his ear.

I get closer and hide behind the sculpture of Venus so I can listen to what he's saying.

"I just need this to be over with." He sighs with exasperation, bringing a hand to his head. "I know. I know, and yes, I'm grateful to work for a man like Lucca Dyshekov, or I'd be fucking screwed."

What is he talking about?

Wait… I know the name he mentioned—Lucca Dyshekov.

Where did I hear it, though?

I think about it, picking my brain apart as I search.

The name is Russian.

The instant I think that, my memory clicks and I remember something from years ago when Mom was alive. She was talking to Father, and he mentioned that name. I remember.

He said Lucca was the new Pakhan of the Yurkov—as in the Bratva—and therefore an enemy to us.

What the hell is going on?

Lukiyan just said he works for Lucca Dyshekov, but he's supposed to be working for my father.

Unless he's not.

He is half Russian so it could fit and possibly make sense. Does it though?

He just said he works for Lucca Dyshekov. I actually heard him say those words, so there's no guesswork here. It follows then that Lukiyan is working for the Bratva.

"I need everything to go to plan," he continues. "Then I'll kill Emilio for what he did and get the fuck out of here."

I gasp, sucking in a sharp breath, and mindlessly step backward, not even thinking about what I'm doing or where I'm going.

Jesus, Lukiyan just said he's going to kill my father.

I heard that, right?

I didn't make it up or fall asleep and have one of my paranormal experiences.

He did say it as clearly as he said he was working for Lucca Dyshekov.

So, I did hear him perfectly right.

I back right into a vase and it falls to the ground, smashing before I can even catch it to steady it.

The sound pierces the blanket of privacy, and he snaps his head around to look at me.

We stare at each other, and an eerie silence fills the space between us.

It's not quiet and reverent like the awe people usually tend to show when they come into this room because it's filled with original antiquities and pieces of wondrous creation. The silence is filled with tension and terror. The kind of deathly silence a person would experience when they know they're going to be killed.

As Lukiyan stares back at me across the distance, I know he knows I heard what he said on the phone.

He has something on me, and I have something on him.

Except the something I have on him is far darker and more twisted and we're all in danger because he's not who he says he is.

"Persephone—"

I run.

Run away from him again for the second time in the last four hours.

This time I'm running for my life as he follows, chasing me.

Knowing how fast he is pumps more blood into my body, but knowing he could kill me pushes me beyond my limit.

I take the door to the left, going out the side entrance which will lead me to the woods.

The stairs are dark, and again, the lights don't pop on.

I don't let that stop me, though. Hearing the heavy thud of his boots behind me keeps me going, keeps me trying, keeps me fighting for my life.

But then I trip over something when I reach the landing on the next floor, and I fall.

I look back only to see what I tripped over, and my heart stops when the moonlight shines down on Maya's face, her eyes wide and dead.

Blood covers her chest. Jesus, there's so much of it.

A tremor takes me unlike any other, and I rush to her side, gathering her up in my arms.

"Maya," I choke, tears instantly flowing from my eyes when I feel how cold she is.

Her head flops back, and her eyes are still wide and dead. I know she's gone, but I don't want her to be.

She's dead. Maya is dead.

"Maya."

Gunfire answers me, and I realize what's happening. The house is under attack. Just like before.

A gamut of emotions cripple me, but my instinct for survival kicks in and I stand. Just then, a large hand grabs me.

I turn to see Lukiyan, but he catches my throat and presses in the center.

"Mne zhal,'" he says.

I know it's Russian, but of course, I don't know what it means.

My vision blurs when he presses into my skin again, then darkness swallows everything.

I am your Hades.

Those words are the last thing on my mind as I realize what he was trying to tell me.

He is death.

17

LUKIYAN

I realize now that I didn't fuck myself over when I pursued Persephone after coming to New York.

No, it wasn't then.

It happened in Brazil. That night we first met.

That was the moment it happened and set me up for a fall.

She was the wild card the Universe threw at me to screw me over in the worst way possible because no matter what she was never going to be with me.

Now we're here.

She's in the back of my car, unconscious while I'm hightailing it off the grounds of the mansion.

We're fleeing. Narrowly escaping the invaders unnoticed.

I'm doing exactly what Emilio asked me to do—taking his daughter to safety.

More importantly, I'm doing exactly what I would

have done for a woman who feels like mine. Except where we're going, there'll be no one to keep her safe from me.

At least I'm the devil I know.

Those men at the house wouldn't have hesitated to kill her, or take her and use her for leverage then kill her.

I don't know what the fuck is happening back there, but my guess is the assholes from The Order came along, killed the staff, and are now in the house.

It's got to be them. Who else could get onto the grounds of the property and inside the house?

Or rather, who the fuck let them in, in the first place?

Was it another assassination attempt? And another attempt to find the device?

Emilio decided to stay at the hotel tonight. Maybe they didn't know that, or it didn't upset their plans because they were searching around.

Which means they're looking for the device.

Fuck.

That's the fucking least of my worries though, because Persephone heard me talking to Aleksei on the phone.

I slipped up. I might not have shouted my plans from the rooftops, but I was reckless.

I thought she was sleeping. It was late enough, and I thought I was alone.

I went in the hall after speaking to Emilio. I'd already decided I wasn't going to tell him about Persephone's escape attempt, but I was still thinking about what to do with her in case she thought to try it again.

I told him I brought Persephone home because she was

feeling sick. That was how I left my conversation with him, then ended up calling Aleksei.

We were already talking for a couple of hours before Persephone came in the hall and I lost track of my awareness. I should have known better than to do that.

My recklessness stopped me from hearing her come into the hall.

I would have been none the wiser of her presence if she didn't bump into that vase. I wouldn't have known either that the house was under attack.

How the hell did I end up in this mess? And how the fuck am I going to get out of it?

I glance up at the rearview mirror and look at the sleeping maiden curled up on the back seat.

She's not going to be asleep for long. All I did was cut off her airway.

There are no hard and fast rules when you use that technique. A person could be out for a few minutes or a couple of hours.

Regardless of when she wakes, she's truly going to hate me.

I am indeed Hades, stealing Persephone away.

It takes me less than an hour to get to the house on Long Island. In daytime traffic that journey could have easily been double the time.

Thankfully, Persephone has been out cold for the whole journey.

When I park up on the drive, I get out of my car and scoop her up, carrying her in my arms like a newborn baby.

I make my way up the wide stone steps and feel for the keys in my back pocket.

When I find them, I open the door and rush into the house.

Aleksei walks out of the living room, stopping short when his gaze falls on the young woman in my arms.

He looks her over and notices the blood on her chest—Maya's blood.

I met Maya only days ago and immediately liked her. It grieves me that she was murdered in such a way.

"What the fuck happened, Lukiyan?" His eyes snap wide.

At the sound of his voice, Persephone stirs. "Grab me one of the tranqs. Quickly."

I didn't want to drug her, but it's for the best right now.

I need to figure things out before we speak.

Aleksei rushes to get the case of tranquilizers from the kitchen while I take Persephone into the living room.

He hands it to me, and I curse myself even more when I administer the drug into her arm.

As her body goes floppy as if the life has left it, I feel worse.

I hold her against me for a few moments, Aleksei

watching me carefully, observing. I press my lips to her forehead and lay her down on the sofa.

When I look at Aleksei again, he flicks his gaze from her to me.

"The mission's compromised. She heard me talking to you on the phone."

"Fuck."

"I didn't know she was in the room. I had to bring her here. I had to regardless, because the house was under attack."

His eyes bulge and his hand flies up to his head. "What the fuck are you saying to me? Attack?"

"Yes. The Order guys came, and I think they were looking for the device."

"Shit. What are we going to do?"

I shake my head. "I don't know yet. I have to deal with her first." I look at Persephone's petite form, with her hair sprawled out around her like a cape. I feel like shit for this and what I'm about to do next. She's a threat now. A risk. And I have to treat her as such. "Where did you put the ropes?"

LUKIYAN

I know I'm walking a thin line the moment I drive back onto the premises of Emilio's home.

Aleksei and I came up with a sketchy plan that's risky as fuck, but it's something in the interim to cover my ass and still help me get what I came here for.

Blood stains on the front door greet me when I walk into the house. The said door is also hanging off the hinges.

More blood covers the marble floors leading to the kitchen and there are men milling about the place who under normal circumstances would be police, but these are actually Emilio's personal investigation team.

Emilio is standing at the top of the stairs looking haggard, like a man at the end of his days. Yet when he sees me, he rushes down the stairs and hope sparks in his good eye. Even the milky white of his dead eye looks like it has hope too and is pleading with me.

"Please tell me you know where she is," he begs, and I feel like a complete motherfucker. It's not because of him though; it's about her. She's the only reason I'm feeling anything because she's my exception. "Please, Persephone is missing, Lukiyan. The cameras show you coming back here with her, then nothing."

Fuck. Of course, the bastards tampered with the surveillance.

My newly formulated plan enters my mind, and I gear up to initiate it.

"I heard her scream," I begin, and the light of hope fades from his eyes. "Then there was a car driving off the premises. I followed it, but I was too late. I lost it. I don't even know if she was in the car. I was hoping to catch them."

"Oh God."

He believes me.

I'd be a good nominee for an award for best actor of the year, but there's nothing honorable about me.

And the reason everything I just said is risky is because whoever the real enemy is, knows nobody took Persephone. I'm just hoping I left my explanation vague enough to include a variety of possibilities for her disappearance.

"I went to talk to some people I thought could help, but they don't know anything."

"It was The Order." He looks like he's aged again.

"Maybe she got away and they didn't take her." Again I leave it vague with something to make him think. That's exactly what would have happened if I didn't bring her back here.

"I have to find her, regardless."

Antonio and Frankie come out of the other room. When Antonio sees me, his face contorts with fury, and he rushes up to me.

"You motherfucker. Why the fuck did you bring her back here!" the fool shouts, balling his hand into a fist to hit me.

I allow him to come at me, but the punch intended for my face doesn't connect. I step out of the way, so he loses his balance and goes straight into the wall instead.

A growl tears from his throat, and he doubles back, but I stop him in his tracks by slamming him back into the wall.

There's no way anyone can tell me he's distraught because his beloved fiancée is missing.

He's not. What he'll miss if I never release her is the opportunity he could have had by marrying her.

Despite that, the thing getting to me the most about this guy is he's genuinely in love with Persephone. I can't stand that.

I wish I didn't know that part and could only see him for the control freak and bastard he is. But I know he loves her from the look in his eyes every time he sees her, and the possessiveness he shows when it comes to her.

But I'm the same kind of possessive bastard who wants her to be his.

I'm no different. The only real difference between us right now is that I have the girl and he doesn't.

"Break it up now!" Emilio bellows like an animal and grabs me.

"What are you going to do, old man?" Antonio challenges.

Emilio answers him with a punch in his face.

"Remember who you're talking to, *boy*. Now get the fuck out of my sight and off my property."

Antonio looks as shocked as I feel.

"Emilio, I want to find Persephone," he insists.

"No more than me." Emilio bares his teeth like a feral animal. "Now get the fuck out. Frankie, escort him out."

"Sure thing, brother." Frankie nods.

When he takes Antonio, I look back at Emilio.

"Come with me," he says. "Let's talk. For real this time."

I dip my head.

We take the stairs up to his office, where he sits me down.

"I need to find my daughter. I need to. If she managed to get to safety then great. So much the better. If not then I know they'll kill her. If you know anything about the Order, then you know that's what they'll do."

I bite down hard on my back teeth. This pretense is hard, but it's what I must do.

"Yes, they will kill her."

"I want you to look for her. You, personally"

"Me, personally?" I'm curious at his change of attitude.

"You know about The Order, don't you?"

"I know who they are and how they work."

"The Camorra don't have dealings with those people, so I don't know anyone else with knowledge of them. You were able to identify them straightaway. That's the level of expertise I need. I also know you care about my daughter." He says that like it's a statement of fact. Since my heart forbids me to lie or pretend he's wrong, all I can do is stare back at him. "If you didn't, you wouldn't have attacked Antonio when he hurt her. You aren't compromised by whatever is happening here and I think I could trust you to keep her safe. She'll be in danger out there whether they have her or not. I fear if they don't have her, she might have used the opportunity to escape."

"And why do you think she'd want to escape?" I want to hear his reasons from his lips.

"She doesn't want to marry Antonio. The arrangement stopped her from dancing. I'm only considering the possibility that she escaped because she would have called by now."

This is good for me. The fact that he's considering a variety of possibilities gives me some room to work with.

Emilio steeples his fingers and clenches his jaw. "I want to believe she escaped, but even if that's the case, she'll still be in danger and there won't be anyone to protect her. They'll know she's my daughter."

That's exactly why I couldn't allow her to do it in the first place.

"Are you going to give me some pointers on why this is happening?"

"I am." He drags in another breath. "It's happening because I have the plans for a device I want to sell on the black market. At the moment the plans are on a chip. The chip is what they're after."

I didn't know it was just the plans he had. I thought it was the actual thing. "What kind of device is it?"

"It's a hacking device. I don't know how people found out about it, but they did and clearly the only people who could know that about my plans are those who work with me closely."

"I agree. Any idea who that could be?"

"No. I have no idea, but after the attack the other night, I moved the chip from the hotel and brought it here. Whoever did this knew that and they also want me dead too. That makes me think there's a bigger plan at work because it doesn't make sense."

"What are the benefits of your death?"

"It could be anything, but this feels personal and like it's to do with the past."

"What makes you say that?" I considered the possibility but couldn't find a link.

"The past was an inside job." He sighs.

That makes sense now, given who he is. No one is supposed to be able to just walk on to his property and massacre his family, but they did. I just thought they managed to do it, but they had the right kind of help.

"What happened then?"

"Another Capo of mine betrayed me when he was bribed by my enemies. Although I killed him, I've always felt there was someone else involved. I never knew who. That's why I keep tabs on my enemies. These long years have passed by and I still feel I'm missing something. Now I'm here again, in what feels like an unresolved matter."

Maybe the person was waiting for the right opportunity and it's now.

But why?

If Emilio is right, then something must have changed to open the door for the attacks happening now.

"I was supposed to have died with my wife and brother," he adds. "We were all supposed to die."

That suggests unfinished business. "Why didn't you die?"

"I'd just gotten a business call from a client who needed to meet. I must have been gone for ten minutes when Maya called me letting me know what was happening. Persephone and I only made it out because I was able to get back up. I was too late to save my wife and brother. Frankie got shot while he was trying to save them and stop them from taking my other daughter, Athena."

"They took her?" More truth is being revealed. I assumed Athena was saved at the same time as Persephone.

"Yes. I found her weeks later, but she was never the same again. Nothing was ever the same again and it was my fault. That's why I need to find Persephone."

"Where is the chip now?"

Emilio reaches into his pocket and holds it up. I'm amazed that such a small thing can cause all this trouble.

He slips it back in his pocket. "I have a team working on completing the device. It should be ready in three weeks. My associate will be coming then to take it to Prague for sale."

Associate. That piques my interest.

"Who is this associate?"

"His name is Judas Kane."

At the mention of that name, my purpose is renewed and the image of my sister lying dead in a sea of red rose petals floating in her blood floods my mind.

The thirst for revenge fuels me with renewed energy and I remember with perfect clarity why I'm here.

"Have you heard of him?" Curiosity fills his eyes.

"Black market dealer. Yes, I have heard of him." I try to say that with as much calm as possible and leave out the part where I also know that Judas is a contract killer used by those dabbling in the black market.

"Then you must have an idea of how much this chip and the device are worth."

"Yes, I do. Does Judas know what's been happening?" If my goal could be achieved with a phone call to Judas right the fuck now, I'll take it.

"No. He's a man of mystery so not even I can summon him when I want. According to how he works, he's not exactly contactable by phone. We mostly meet in person to discuss business once he's secured a deal, which he already has. So he'll be here in three weeks."

Three weeks it is.

I've waited this long; three weeks will give me time to prepare for war and keep Emilio's ass alive.

"My priority right now is finding my daughter. Please help me find her, Lukiyan." His eyes plead with me.

"Don't worry, I'll do my best."

I pick up the fake passport Persephone had in her duffle bag and look at it. I saw it last night amongst the other things she got.

She changed her name to Belinda Fairchild. Nice name but I like Persephone Vittorio more.

She has everything in this bag to start a new life.

Her plan to escape was well thought through and someone helped her big time.

I considered that it could have been Raven, but I don't think it was.

Persephone is a clever girl. She wouldn't have risked telling Raven because she's the first person people would question.

This plan of hers was completely covert, so whoever helped her was impartial enough to get away with doing things under wraps.

Still, if she'd disappeared at the fundraiser, no one would be any wiser.

I don't know where she was going, but it doesn't matter now.

She's here with me.

That's as far as I've reached in my plan. I don't know the next step and now she's here and not out in the world like everyone believes, I have to be more careful.

I just got back from Emilio's. Persephone is still asleep.

I tied her up because I need her to fear me. She needs to understand the gravity of her part in the situation, and the risk she is to me.

I need her to understand that we aren't the same people we were when she wanted me to fuck her.

Everything has changed now.

Well... not everything.

I'm still just as fascinated with her as I ever was.

I won't be the fool and lie to myself. Part of me wants this because it's a way to keep her with me for a little longer. I don't know how long, but I can't release her any time soon.

I'm supposed to be off duty for the next four days, but now that I'm *looking* for Persephone, I'll need to check in with Emilio and make it look like I'm doing my best to find her.

That will only work for so long. I'm hoping I can stretch it out for three weeks.

After that, I'll still have Persephone to worry about.

Despite what I've made her believe, or what I need her to believe, I'm not going to hurt her. I couldn't, no matter whose daughter she is.

I know that's irony at its finest, since I've kidnapped her.

The bright sunlight beaming through the floor-to-ceiling glass windows of my father's former office shines down on me as I lean against the desk and gaze out to the sea.

It feels weird being in this house without my family. I've been here a few times since their deaths but the emptiness always compels me to cut my visits short.

Although this house was a base for business, my father always brought us here on vacation in the summer and sometimes for the thanksgiving and Christmas holidays. He liked New York. I liked it too because it was far away from where I grew up.

It was in this house, in this same room, that he first told me I could call him my father and I did. It was easy because I never had one and Melissa automatically called our adopted parents mom and dad. It was harder for me, but felt right.

This house has been in his family for generations. The staff who worked for my father are still here and maintain the place.

If my father had other family this house would have passed to them. But, like all his other assets, it belongs to me. The net worth of everything combined is something in the range of a billion dollars.

I'm a rags-to-riches story, but no one would ever guess that because of the work I do. And nobody truly knows me.

Aleksei walks into the room as I put the passport back in the bag.

"You're back. Did they believe you?" He gives me a pensive stare.

"They did." As far as I know for now. "Emilio also thinks Persephone might have escaped on her own."

"That's good for us."

"It is because Judas is coming in three weeks."

His face brightens. "You're kidding. When did you find that out?"

"Emilio told me. So we have to wrap this up by then. I need to get to Judas the first chance I get."

"I'll continue monitoring the calls so we know the moment he arrives in New York."

"Thanks. Can you also do a deeper check on everyone who works for Emilio. He said the massacre in the past was an inside job and thinks the latest attack could be the same person."

"If it is, does he have any idea why they'd come back now? That happened four years ago."

"He doesn't know."

"Okay, I'll look into it. What about the girl?"

I take a moment to think. "Leave her to me."

I glance at the clock on the wall across from us. It's just eleven.

My little houseguest should be waking up soon.

19

PERSEPHONE

Lush green grass covers the meadow like a blanket.

It's absolutely beautiful, but then Brazil is always amazing at this time of year. And every other time of year I've been here.

Athena is off in the distance, walking toward the river.

Her hair lifts in the wind, and when she turns to face me, she smiles and

beckons for me to follow.

I do, running toward her.

"Wait for me!" I call out.

"Always."

I reach her, and she touches my face with cold, clammy hands.

They're so cold I shiver.

"Where are we going today?" I ask as she takes both my hands and starts skipping in a circle.

"Anywhere you want. You just have to wake up."

"I'm awake."

"No. Wake up, Persephone. Don't let him kill you."

"Kill me?"

She stops, plants a kiss on my forehead, and when she pulls away, her head is covered with blood and a massive hole is blown into her skull. Her eyes are pale white and dead.

She's dead.

Just like Maya.

"Wake up."

My eyes snap open, but there's nothing but darkness all around me.

Frantically, I look around and try to remember what happened.

I contemplate the possibility of death, but death doesn't feel like this.

This is something else that's just as sinister.

Where am I?

The coldness against my cheek suggests I'm on the floor. A stone floor like the basement at home.

I try to move, but all I can do is wiggle my body. My hands and feet are bound with something tight, like... rope?

Is that rope binding me?

I manage to shuffle until I'm sitting, and when I lean, my back hits a wall.

There's a sliver of light piercing through a tiny hole across from me, and the sound of waves beyond the walls.

Where the hell am I?

Everything is so fuzzy, and the darkness doesn't help.

Closing my eyes, I will myself to focus and try to remember.

What happened, Persephone? How'd you get here?

Where is here?

The dream comes back to me and, suddenly, the memory of Maya's cold, dead, bleeding body ravages my mind.

The memory assaults my soul, then everything else follows in the same brutal malevolent manner.

Lukiyan.

Oh my God. He took me. I remember him grabbing me after I found Maya, then there was darkness.

Now I'm still in darkness and he's locked me away from the light.

I am your Hades.

Those words come back to me again, like a wicked, evil taunt.

He kidnapped me.

Did he kill Maya?

Oh my God.

Maya. I'm so sorry. That shouldn't have happened to you.

She deserved better than a death like that. I think she was shot.

What about me now?

I have no idea where I am and I'm helplessly bound, with no way of escape.

I can't believe that I fought so hard to be free. Now look at me.

And Lukiyan, he's going to kill my father. Has he done so already?

Please, God, no.

"Lukiyan!" I call out his name in anguish like a wild animal trapped in a snare.

I don't know if it's a good or bad idea to call for him, but he's the only person who can give me answers. Even if it's just to tell me whether my father is still alive.

"Lukiyan, let me go!" I scream.

There's nothing but a deadly silence, and I wonder if I'm truly alone in this place, sitting on the floor with my hands and feet tied up.

"Lukiyan!"

This time, footsteps sound on a hard floor, then a door ahead opens, bringing in daylight.

An overhead light switches on, making the room a fraction brighter, then I see him.

"You monster!"

"Easy, tiger."

I'm looking at the man I gave so much to, and I'm having a hard time believing he's the same guy. He's not, and that's the point. He was never who I thought he was.

"Did you kill my father?"

"Not yet."

My heart squeezes. "But you're going to?"

"Let's get this straight. You need to listen to me." He speaks in a low, cool tone that makes my nerves scatter. "Can you listen to me?"

"I want you to let me go." My glare intensifies.

"Baby, I can't do that."

Because I heard something I shouldn't have.

"Did you kill Maya?" That had to be his doing.

"No. Those were different men. They were at the house for another reason."

"What reason?"

"Let's just say I'm not the only one who wants your father dead."

He walks closer and crouches down next to me.

"Princess—"

"Don't fucking call me that." Tears stream out the corners of my eyes. When he touches my cheek to wipe them, I flinch and try to move away, but it's fruitless. "Who the hell are you? You're in the Bratva, aren't you?"

A touch of a smile lifts his lips. "How did you guess?"

"Lucca Dyshekov. He's your Pakhan."

"Clever girl."

"Who are you? And don't give me any bullshit."

"I am who I say I am, just not what I am."

"You lying bastard."

"I never lied to you. Not once."

I don't know why, but the admission makes my temper flare. He's right. He didn't lie to me, not once. Not even about being my Hades.

He just never said anything and avoided all the important questions.

I remember when I asked him about working for my father. I had a feeling something was off with his answer. This was fucking why.

I knew all along, but I didn't want to believe it because of how I felt about him.

"We were never a coincidence, were we?" I challenge.

He sighs and lifts a lock of my hair. My heartbeat kicks up a notch.

"I think we were more like an anomaly. I didn't know who you were in Brazil. That part just happened, and I can't explain it any more than you can. I didn't know who you were until a few weeks ago, but it didn't matter. It wasn't going to stop me from doing what I have to do."

"You need to let me go. How can you treat me like this?" How can he when he saved me from Antonio?

"I don't mean to, but letting you go is not an option when you could jeopardize my plans. You know why I'm here now and what I want to do."

"Please don't hurt my father. Please don't. Don't kill him. I beg of you."

"Persephone. Your father is a very bad man."

Don't I know that? Look what happened to Mom, and Athena prior to her death. No matter how much help my father's enemies had, what happened was his fault.

"What did he do to you?"

"He's part of the reason why my sister is dead."

"Your sister?"

"Her name was Melissa and she had a bright future ahead of her. We had a hard life growing up so that was a big deal for her. First your father turned her into a whore, then he hooked her up with the crazy motherfucker who killed her and her unborn baby. She was only seventeen when he ruined her."

A shudder runs through me and my eyes widen.

My father did that?

"I'm sorry. I'm sorry about your sister."

"It's his price to pay. Men like him don't care. They just sign up the next body who can fulfill a duty. So he's as good as dead to me. I'm just biding time. He'll lead me to my sister's killer and I'll kill them both."

"What about me? Are you going to kill me too?"

Would he kill me?

Lukiyan stands and raw fear rips me apart. My throat works but it's dry.

"Lucky for you, I still want you."

More tears tip over my lids. "You can't keep me here."

"We will see about that."

His long, athletic legs carry him away from me and as he proceeds up the stairs, doom settles in the pit of my stomach.

20

PERSEPHONE

It feels like I've been in my new prison for eons.

At least Lukiyan left the light on and I'm not in the darkness like before.

I've kept an eye on the little light peeking through the hole in the wall, trying to guess what time it could be. It hasn't started to fade yet, so I assumed it's still early in the day.

The sound of the waves has stilled though.

They were my only distraction from my worries and terror. I think I should be hungry or thirsty but I'm not. It's probably a good thing because I might need to use the bathroom and there are no facilities down here. Just the gray floor.

I've been mulling over everything Lukiyan told me, and thinking about what I'm going to do.

Or rather, what he might do to me.

He's going to kill my father and I can't stop it from happening.

It will happen.

Then what?

Once whatever interest Lukiyan has in me fades, he'll have no further use for me.

Realistically though, he already has no use for me because I'm a loose end that needs to be tied up.

When I think of my father my heart squeezes with so much disappointment.

My father's dirty business dealings have never been something I overlooked. I always knew we were a crime family who dealt with shady shit, but what he did to Lukiyan's sister is inexcusable. She was younger than me, much younger.

I can't imagine Father doing what he did to a young girl, but I know it's true.

There's no question about truth here when I know what the men in the Circle are like. So why should my father be any different?

I also know about the prostitution ring, so... what defense is there?

Father has his shortcomings with me, he deceived me when it came to Antonio, didn't fight for my career when he knew how much it meant to me, and we've had a rocky relationship, especially since Athena died.

He helped ruin me and truth be told, he helped push me into this situation I'm in now.

But that doesn't mean I want him to die.

Whatever is left of my heart has always remembered him as the father who helped create the magic Mom made for us when Athena and I were kids.

He was the person who took me to my first ballet class and he never missed a show. Not once, from the smallest performance to the biggest—even when things were bad with us.

I remember him as the man who saved me when everyone else was being slaughtered during the massacre.

The terror I experienced that day was so overwhelming.

My body was so weak at that point that breathing hurt and so did living, but I didn't want to die.

Mom and Athena made me their priority and got me to the safe room.

I wish with all my heart they'd stayed with me. But they went to help the servants. There were maids there with babies and children. There were also older people who wouldn't have been able to escape an attack without assistance.

With the sound of gunfire all around me all I could do was pray that we'd all make it through and some miracle would happen. But all those people were butchered that day.

I didn't know Father had gone out because we were all in the family room watching a movie.

When he came back he went straight to the safe room because that's where we were told to go in case of trouble. He expected to find the three of us inside but only found me. I was so happy to see him. I just thought he'd fix everything because that's what he always did.

It was while he was carrying me out of the room that a man stabbed him in the eye. He killed the man but it was one more thing that slowed him down from getting to Mom.

Just as we got to her, someone shot her straight in her heart. I don't even know who fired the bullet. I just remember screaming and crying.

I'll never forget how Father cried.

It was the first time I'd ever witnessed him cry and his tears were that of a shattered soul who'd lost everything.

On top of that, those men took Athena. That was another disaster we had to live through but Father didn't sleep until he found her.

What happened last night was like déjà vu, and there's more to come.

I love my father, and that's why I can't let him die, even if he deserves to.

I just can't allow that to happen to him, and if there's something I can do, I'll do it.

Footsteps sound on the floor outside the door and my body tenses.

Is that Lukiyan coming back?

The steps sound different to his. He has a heavier foot-fall. That doesn't mean it's not him now. He could be wearing different shoes.

The door opens and my gaze lands on a man the same

height and build as Lukiyan, but with fewer tattoos. They also look similar in age.

He comes down the stairs and I take note of the tattoos on his forearms which are unmistakably Russian.

When he reaches me he flicks a knife and I gasp, wondering if he's going to use it on me.

"Relax, if we wanted you dead, you'd already know," he speaks with an unmistakable hint of a Russian accent.

"Who are you?"

He shakes his head. "Sorry sweetheart. No names yet."

Of course. How stupid of me.

"Where is Lukiyan? If that's really his name."

He chuckles. "It is, and he'll be with you shortly. Your room is ready."

"Room? How nice of you. The prisoner gets a room."

"And food too." Sarcasm laces through his words. "But if you piss me off, you're staying down here in the dark. Understand?"

I can already see this man is just as ruthless as Lukiyan —or worse—so I decide to play this sensibly.

"I understand."

"Hold out your hands."

I do and he cuts the rope away. I realize this was a strategy to keep me in line. Keep me afraid.

It worked.

He undoes the ropes around my feet next and puts out a hand to help me stand.

I take his calloused hand and as I push to my feet, my

legs give out from the blood rushing back. He catches me, steadying me, then ushers me out of the room.

When we get to the top of the stairs the sight that greets me steals my breath away.

There's an entire glass wall running down the long hallway ahead of us.

Outside is the perfect view of bright sunlight hitting the rolling waves of the sea.

I guess from the beautiful scenery we must be some-where near the Hamptons, or near a beach on Long Island. I can't be sure.

We walk down the corridor and go through a set of glass panel doors that open for us automatically.

There I'm immersed in more beauty as we walk into a hall filled with paintings like the ones back home. These have more landscapes though.

The décor is ornate, with gold and burgundy colors. There are antique-looking items everywhere, from the furniture to the fixtures on the walls.

"Lukiyan lives here?" I mutter.

"It's one of his homes."

One of his homes?

My God.

He was never a simple bodyguard.

This man didn't need a good job that paid well.

He has all of this and probably never needed anything. Maybe he never needed me either.

Was anything ever real with him?

The man leads me to a set of grand stairs that have

gold leaf accents along the banister and up we go, taking the wide marble steps until we reach the second floor. There I'm taken to a beautiful room which has an elderly lady inside folding the sheets on the queen-size bed in the center.

Her face brightens when we walk in, but she doesn't quite smile.

She looks Russian and speaks it to the man. He answers and she returns her gaze to me with a warmth in her eyes that I foolishly find solace in.

There is nothing here for me, so nothing can comfort me.

How can it when I don't know what's going on?

"I am Lina, I am the head maid here. I will take care of you." Her accent is still quite thick. I have to really focus to understand what she's saying. "So if you need anything, please ask."

"Thank you."

"I'll leave you two to talk." The man focuses on me. "I'm sure I don't have to tell you not to try anything foolish. The place is heavily guarded and there's no one around but us for miles."

I don't answer, he knows I'm helpless as shit so I won't give him the pleasure of being some subservient.

He backs out the door and leaves us.

"There are some clothes there." Lina points to a stack of clothes I recognize as mine. They're what I packed and put in my duffle bag. I don't see the bag anywhere though.

"Where's my bag?"

"I don't know. This is what Master Romanechka left for you."

Bastard, he took my bag and went through it. I have personal things in there that are dear to me. Things Athena gave me, and Mom too. I have family pictures and my dancing certificates. All things money can't buy or replace.

"If you want to shower and change go ahead. I've made lunch already so I'll bring that up for you."

"Thank you." I sound scarily calm.

I've learned that there's no point making an enemy out of those trying to help you.

I wouldn't do it anyway, when my staff were so special to me. Staff like Maya were like family.

Tears prick at my eyes when I think of her. I can't believe she's dead, and if I hadn't gone back to the house, I'd never know. I'd still think she was alive.

Lina leaves. When she closes the door I expect her to lock it but she doesn't.

It means nothing though because this fancy room is still part of the prison.

I look around at the four salmon walls and the painting of somewhere snowy near the window bay.

I want to scream at the nothingness and the way the situation has been forced on me.

What does Lukiyan seriously want me to do now?

Act normal and pretend things are okay?

Where the fuck is he?

Where would he have gone?

And is this his bedroom?

Looking around again, I decide it's too girly and doesn't feel like him.

I walk around looking at the books on the shelf in the corner, which has fairytales, only fairytales.

On the chest of drawers is a set of porcelain ballerinas and another set of fairies. This is definitely a girl's room.

I decide to do a little more snooping but find the wardrobes and cupboards empty.

Lina comes back with a tray of delicious food I want to refuse or throw out the window but I think better of both options.

I'm actually starving. I didn't eat yesterday because I was so nervous, and what I did manage to stuff down was just a few grapes at the fundraiser.

If I'm to confront Lukiyan I need my strength. So when she leaves me again, I eat.

She made a chicken casserole with boiled rice and spring vegetables. On the side is a slice of chocolate cake and some macaroons.

Once I'm done I shower and stay under the cold spray of water for a long time before I get out and put on something similar to what I was wearing previously.

Then I wait.

Night falls and I'm still waiting.

I'm propped in the window bay going crazy with worry.

I'm almost relieved when I hear footsteps and I know it's him before the door opens and he enters.

Pulling in a deep breath, I push to my feet and bring my hands together, staring at him with anticipation.

I'm not sure who's going to talk first. Him or me.

I don't want to go first, because all I can do is beg and I loathe looking pathetic.

Pathetic is all I seem to have been for years as one thing after another happened to me. Nevertheless, waiting for him to speak is torture.

"What are you planning to do to me?" My voice comes out raspy.

"Not sure yet." His eyes fall up and down my body and I feel like I'm naked, although I'm fully clothed.

He glances at the tray and takes note of the empty plates which look like they've been licked clean, then looks back at me.

"You ate. Good."

"Where am I?"

His lips twitch at my curiosity. "Long Island."

"And this is one of your homes?"

"It is." He comes closer but not too close.

I'm glad because being in the same room as him is already too much.

"Where do you normally live?"

"L.A. This place belonged to my adopted father."

"You were adopted?" That's why I couldn't tell what he was.

"Yes. My sister and I were adopted."

"Whose room is this?" My gaze darts from him to the porcelain ballerinas on the chest of drawers.

"My sister used to use it when we came here on vacation."

"Where are your parents?"

"They're all dead. Everyone I call family is dead now."

There's a moment of that awful silence I hate, and I can't think of anything other than what I want from him.

"Lukiyan, my father is many things," I begin, schooling my worry. "You know the kind of world we come from. Nevertheless, he was wrong for what he did to your sister. He was really wrong, because whatever he did led to her death. But I'm begging you not to kill him."

He keeps his eyes riveted to mine.

"Do you expect me to just agree because you beg me?"

No. I didn't expect it, but I hoped for it. "He's my father. Can't we talk about it?"

"If he's just as responsible for my sister's death as her killer is, what do we have to talk about?"

"I'll do anything," I cut in before he can continue. "Anything. Just don't kill him."

Wild desire darkens his bright blue eyes. His gaze pierces through me and I wish he would say something.

"Sweet Persephone, you would do *anything* to save your old man?"

"Wouldn't you do anything to save a member of your family you loved?"

"I would." Something comes into his eyes that gives me a glimpse of him. It shows me that he knows exactly what I mean because he would have done anything to save his sister, and this is his version of saving her soul.

"If you would do anything, my offer shouldn't be a surprise to you."

"Except, I don't think you know what the hell it means to offer a man like me *anything*."

He takes another two steps and the look in his eyes now tells me I might have hope. I just might have reached him in some way.

An idea forms when a spark invades his hard gaze and I recognize the sexual haze filling his eyes.

How many times have I seen this man look at me like that and know he wants me?

He even said it.

He did.

So what I'm thinking now goes against everything I want, but what I wanted went to hell a long time ago.

"I know what I'm doing."

He inches closer. "And what do you think I want, Persephone?"

The same thing Hades wanted. "Me."

He recoils and his expression takes on a hardness which confuses me.

The desire in his eyes dims as he inclines his head, and the twitch of his lips is the only thing that tells me he's considering my offer.

"You? You're giving yourself to me."

"My life for his."

"But you wanted freedom."

"I don't want my father to die."

"Do you understand what you're offering me?"

"I do." I nod, as if that will make him believe me even more.

He stares at me for a long moment as if he's trying to figure me out. The waiting and suspense is more torture my mind can't endure.

"Do you accept or not?" I feel like a cheap whore begging for a fuck.

"I think I might need something more to persuade me before I agree to anything. This is, after all, quite a big deal on my part."

On his part?

What an asshole. I just offered my life in exchange for my father's and he doesn't see that as a big deal?

I suppose he can think whatever he wants since I'm the one who's begging here. And since I am, I need to continue begging.

"What do I have to do to persuade you, Lukiyan?"

"Fuck me."

21

PERSEPHONE

I'm held captive by his ruthless stare and his fierce beauty as the sharp pang of reality coils through my insides.

What did I really think he was going to say to me?

Or, want to do to me.

This shouldn't actually be a surprise, but I'm still thrown off kilter.

Yes, I knew he'd want sex. The way he looked at me was a pretty good clue. And why wouldn't he since we've already done it?

I guess I'm stunned because I never felt like a slut when we had our one-night stand in Brazil. I never felt like a whore until just now.

Trust came easier when I didn't know him. Now I know the fraud he is, I'm supposed to fuck him without knowing if he's going to accept my offer, or play me for the innocent fool again.

"Having second thoughts, Princess?" A devilish look

enters his eyes and he gives me a mocking smirk as he reaches out to touch my cheek.

"No, I'm not."

"Alright, then take your clothes off and get on the bed."

The reason I'm doing this pushes to the front of my mind so I swallow my pride and start taking off my clothes.

When he looks at my naked body with that need in his eyes, I'm taken back to the people we were in Brazil, and I feel like a traitor for wanting him.

We aren't those people anymore.

I'm not that girl anymore if I just offered my body to him so he would spare my father's life.

"Good girl. Now get on the bed with your ass up."

I walk over to the bed, and he follows. His footsteps sound so loud in my ears, like rounds of thunder clashing against a tempestuous sea.

He lands a heavy hand on my ass when I get on the bed on my hands and knees. At that moment, I stop thinking and start feeling.

Like a dark shadow, he hovers over me. I can just about see him in the long mirror across from us, so I try to keep my eyes on him, on his next move.

He plants one finger on my clit and starts rubbing in circles, coaxing the arousal out of me.

"Your pussy is so wet. You're begging to be fucked. Looks like this was the perfect excuse, right?"

I snap my gaze around to him and scowl. "Fuck you, you fucking asshole. You know why I'm doing this."

"I do. You're doing this because you want me just as much as I want you. Your sweet cunt doesn't lie."

I want to tell him he's wrong, but he plunges two fingers into my pussy and a desperate moan pours from my throat instead.

I'm trying to hold on to some sense of dignity, but it doesn't work. We both know I'm wet because I want him, but it's only me who feels like a slut.

He starts pumping in and out of my passage and his deep thrusts sends shockwaves to my pussy.

The pleasurable wave explodes with the sensation and a savage orgasm claims me as mercilessly as he is.

As I try to catch my breath and compose myself, he moves to my side.

Grabbing my left nipple, he squeezes, pinching the taut peak until it hardens painfully. Then he runs something cold and metallic over my back. I glance in the mirror and the breath leaves my body when I see he's holding a knife.

Terror moves me away from him but he grabs my arm and holds me in place.

"What are you going to do to me!" *My God, he's crazy.*

Is he going to kill me?

Is that what he's going to do?

Am I some kind of joke to him?

"Sweet Persephone, it's only fair you know what kind of man you're offering yourself to." He runs the blade over my skin again. This time using the sharp edge.

"I told you, I just want to save my father."

"So the only way you see out of this is to offer your

soul to the devil?" He makes a tsking sound. "Poor, sweet, little one. You'll truly do anything for your father."

"Yes. Please... don't kill him." All the bravado I had moments ago is replaced by fear. "Lukiyan, please don't kill me," I add in a mere whisper.

"I told you, I want you. I've never wanted anything more than you." A chaste kiss is planted on the top of my head and the knife clatters to the floor.

Before I can process the meaning of his words or his next move, he goes back to my pussy and licks over my folds.

Circling his tongue around my swollen clit, he pleases my sensitive nub, then plunges deep inside me, making my core light up with delicious fire. He eats me out like an exquisite meal, coaxing me to orgasm once more.

A flood of pleasure rips through me and I come viciously.

"God!" I dig my toes into the mattress and grind my pussy over his face.

I can't think beyond the way he's making me feel. Everything is slipping away from me and I didn't know it was possible for this to feel better than the last time.

Moving up my body, he presses warm lips to my ear and licks over the lobe. "You're going to scream for me, Persephone. Scream my name."

I look over my shoulder at him as he backs away to shove his pants down his hips, freeing his cock.

I can see from the pre-cum leaking from the tip of the

bulbous head and the dark shade of the pulsing veins along his shaft that he's straining.

Giving me no time to recover from the wild orgasm he just gave me, Lukiyan rolls on a condom, grabs my hips, and thrusts into my pussy.

My body, soaking wet and ready for him welcomes his length but the force with which he thrusts in makes me shiver to my core.

I cry out a sound of unmistakable ecstasy and beneath the drumming of my heart I hear his deep chuckle.

"That's right, Princess. Scream for me."

Pleasure paralyzes my entire being and all I can do is grasp on to the silky sheets to stop myself from collapsing.

Lukiyan thrusts deeper and harder and harder, speeding up in a vicious rhythm that feels like rage.

I remember thinking the same thing that night he came into my room and punished my mouth with his cock. It's worse now.

Anger has turned to wrath and he's fucking me like he wants to punish me and teach me a lesson.

Deep down I know what it is.

I knew what it was that night too. It was the no-names hookup we had in Brazil, finding out who I was, and that I was engaged.

Tonight it's because he wants to kill my father, and I'm giving him the last thing I have left so he doesn't.

There's a new roughness to his grip on my hips. Then he slaps my ass so hard I feel the sting deep down in my core.

While flames continue to consume me, he spanks me again, taking me deeper into that dark place where I'm at the edge. As I fall over the precipice I scream.

He fucks me faster, driving deeper into my body relentlessly at an aggressive pace that knows no limit. The lines between pleasure and pain blur into one and I realize with disgust that I like this.

I like what he's doing to me.

I like his aggression, and the savage side of him that's raw and dominant.

What does that say about me and who I thought I was?

Or what I thought I'd like.

This is wrong. It's so very wrong, but my body is luxuriating in the sensation of him.

Everything he's done and what he's made me resort to should destroy the feelings I have for him.

But… I'm that fucked up that I still want him.

In my heart, I know I like what he's doing to me because this maleficent devil wants to break me to get to the parts of me I keep hidden from the world.

Only he knows how to reach those parts. Only he has seen them.

Pleasure and pain can't be the same, but it is with him.

And I love it more than I should.

"Scream my name, Princess. Let me hear you say my name." He digs his fingers into my skin and I scream again.

"Luki—yan!

My cries bounce off the walls in the room and the walls of my soul.

Another wild orgasm hits and I'm wrecked.

Ruined and broken with nothing left but helplessness.

In the prison of his hold I pray I've been the best version of the whore he turned me into and I've *persuaded* him.

He's still moving inside me, still fucking me, still arousing me.

Then finally his relentless pounding stops and the deep male rumble of his groan rips through the air. He climaxes, flooding me with warmth I can feel through the condom.

When he stills, he pulls out of me and we fall on to the bed in a sweaty heap.

He slips an arm around me and pulls me closer, pressing his lips to my ear again. "Alright, Persephone Vittorio… I accept your offer."

PERSEPHONE

Bright sunlight spilling through the window wakes me from a deep slumber.

I shield my eyes with the back of my hand and prop myself up onto my elbows.

Glancing down at myself I wince when I see I'm lying on top of the bed naked, without so much as a sheet covering me.

I sit up, feeling the soreness between my thighs and instantly vivid memories of how ruthlessly Lukiyan claimed me fill my mind.

We had sex two more times after he accepted my offer. Those times were just as rough as the first time, with the absence of the knife.

Last night was darker than the first time we were together.

I went over a line I didn't even know existed for me to

cross and relished in his touch, savoring his name on my lips as I called out for him again and again.

Reaching for the cool silk sheets, I cover myself and look around the room, my gaze falling on the salmon walls then the white door leading into the ensuite.

I listen carefully to see if he's in there, but I don't think he is.

There's no sound coming from inside, so I'm alone.

I release a labored sigh and bring my hand to my head.

What am I doing?

What am I actually doing?

This is my version of doing anything to save my father, and Lukiyan accepted.

I should feel more relieved. I am, but I truly feel like I've sold my soul to the devil.

And was it enough to save my father?

I don't know.

Maybe it saved him from Lukiyan but what about these other people?

There's still missing information I need answers to.

With that in mind I get off the bed, take a quick shower then go downstairs.

I already know it must be close to lunchtime before I catch a glimpse of the grandfather clock in the living room.

A delicious aroma envelopes me when I turn the corner and find Lina in the kitchen with two younger maids who smile at me. Both look similar and have dark hair. They also look like they couldn't be that much older than me.

"Morning," Lina greets me.

"Morning to you all." I acknowledge the three women with a smile.

"These are my daughters, Vanessa and Colleen." She points at them respectively. "They don't speak English very well but they understand you."

"Good to meet you," I say. They seem nice and it is good in general to meet people with smiling faces, but the situation is at odds with why I'm here.

Surely they must know I'm a prisoner, but perhaps they're used to that sort of thing. The only other men I know who are as ruthless as those in the Camorra are the Bratva. So, I'm certain these ladies have seen the dark side.

"I've made brunch," Lina states proudly, pointing to the oven. "I hope you like lasagna."

"I love it."

"Fantastic. Have something to eat then I'll give you the tour of the house and the grounds."

Clearly she's been given her orders.

"Where is Lukiyan?"

"He's working."

Working? What exactly does that mean?

And who is he working for?

"When is he going to be back?"

"Probably by dinner time."

Great. I have to wait again.

"Take a seat and I'll serve you up some food."

Again I feel like I'm going to rip my skin off and Hulk out from the torture, but I take a seat at the breakfast table and keep my cool.

I'm given the tour of the place which takes a little over two hours.

On the surface, at least it gave us something to do. Beneath that, I think Lina was entrusted with the task of watching me.

I'm impressed and surprised at how big the house is and the vast landscape which includes a private beach.

The house is also heavily guarded just like I was told.

Any fleeting thoughts I might have had about escaping flew right out of my mind the moment I saw what I was up against.

The tour ends at the rose garden we started with which is just by the terrace.

We sit around the little wicker table and Vanessa brings us a tray with a pitcher of lemonade and some chocolate chip cookies.

She pours us both a glass of lemonade then heads back into the house.

"How long have you worked here?" I rest my hands in my lap.

Lina smiles proudly. "Forty years. I actually grew up here on these grounds. My family have always worked for the Kozlovs."

"Kozlov?" I think for a moment and remember Lukiyan is adopted.

Lina looks a little thrown off guard and I guess that maybe she shouldn't have told me that.

"Yes."

"It's okay, Lukiyan told me he was adopted."

Relief washes over her face. "Ahh, good. Kozlov was his adopted father's surname. Lukiyan kept Romanechka out of respect to his birth mother. It was also a way to remember her. He... thought nobody would remember her otherwise. That was his way of keeping her memory alive."

It's strange, I feel like we could be talking about two different people.

"That's really sweet." And now I'm wondering about his real mother.

"He knew his birth mother?"

"Yes. She died when he was twelve and after that he and his sister were adopted by the Kozlovs."

Last night when he said everyone died, he really did mean that. It's sad. It's good though that he got to go to a family with his sister. I'm guessing she would have been around five at the time. Some of the people in the circle I know who have adopted wanted babies. It's touching when people adopted older kids and go so far as to keep siblings together.

"The Kozlovs sound like good people."

"They were." She nods.

Good, but their son is one ruthless bastard.

Still, I've only been given dribs and drabs of his story, and all that I've been told has given me a glimpse of the monster behind the man.

Death can do that to a person—*turn him into a monster.*

I finish my lemonade and we start eating the cookies, while Lina talks about Russia.

I'm fascinated, until I see the man from yesterday approaching us.

Instantly I straighten up, on guard, remembering not to get comfortable.

He dips his head at Lina then looks at me. "Lukiyan wants to see you. I will take you to his office."

He's back.

Thank God I don't have to wait until late tonight, but something tells me I'm in for another round of crazy when I go to that office.

23

PERSEPHONE

The man escorts me back into the house.

"Is it time to give me a name yet?" I ask him when we step on to the corridor from yesterday. "I can't come up with anything for you, except 'the man'."

He cuts me a sidelong glance and I think he's going to ignore me until his lips quirk into a brief smile.

"It's Aleksei."

"Well now I have a name." I don't know why I'm bothering to be pleasant. It's not going to change my situation one way or another.

They're not going to let me go.

We approach a large oak door which Aleksei opens.

Lukiyan is inside, leaning over a grand mahogany desk like the one in my father's office at home.

Home...

I was always going to miss home, but now I miss it even more, and the people inside that I love.

Aleksei leaves us and closes the door.

Lukiyan straightens and gazes at me with those piercing eyes as if he's undressing me.

"Good sleep?" He studies my face with an amused expression.

"I slept." The quality of my sleep is none of his concern. "Did you go back to my house?"

"Yes."

"Are my father and family okay? Did… anyone else die?" I hate the quiver of emotion in my voice.

"Your father is fine. A few of your guards are dead, and Maya was the only maid who was killed."

My heart shrinks away at the thought of anyone dying, but Maya… I'm so torn. I never realized when I said goodbye that morning she was going to die.

"What do those people want? Why did that happen?" I'm afraid to ask if my father has done something else in case Lukiyan remembers his own vendetta and changes his mind about our agreement.

"They want your father dead, and they're looking for something valuable he possesses."

There's always something to worry about. Father has a lot of valuable possessions. "What is it?"

"Let's not talk about that."

I grit my teeth and decide there are more important things to ask. "What does my father think happened to me?" *Does he even care?*

He knew I was at the house because one of the guards

saw me go inside with Lukiyan. The cameras would have also picked us up going through the front doors.

"He thinks you've either been taken, or that you used the chance to escape because you didn't want to marry Antonio." He blinks, looking fascinated.

This must be perfect for him. My father is no fool. It takes a lot for him to go on assumptions, so Lukiyan deserves an award.

"Is he even looking for me?"

"Of course he is." He gives me an incredulous glare. "You're his heir. He has every reason to want to look for you, and he's asked yours truly to find you."

"You?" This really is some joke. My father tasked my captor with finding me because he believes someone else kidnaped me, or that I escaped.

"Me, indeed."

"You must be loving this. Are you just going to pretend you're looking for me?"

"I'm a busy man, Persephone Vittorio. I have better things to do than pretend. My sister's killer will be here in three weeks' time, and since your father is my link, I'll try to keep him alive until then."

"What?" My brows snap together in confusion.

"Try to keep up, Princess. Your father just gained an extra pair of hands to help him catch the men who want him dead." He walks up to me and leans in so we're eye to eye. "He has one of the most deadliest assassins in the Bratva working for him and he doesn't even know it."

My lips part and the blood siphons from my body.

Assassin.

That's what Lukiyan is?

Only someone like that would think it was okay to kidnap me, run a knife over my naked body, then fuck me to prove myself to him.

"Are you scared yet, Princess?" he intones and I remember with perfect clarity that he said those same words to me back in Brazil.

At the time, I'd said no.

But I'm scared now so I don't answer.

He brushes over my cheek. "Too pretty to die yet."

And he's too pretty to live.

"What happens if you don't stop the people in three weeks?"

He smiles. "Then your father has a serious problem."

And Father could still end up dead. What a fucking mess.

I don't think there's anything more to do than what I've done. Realistically though, my father is one of the heads of the Camorra, he should be able to stop these people. The past shouldn't have happened either.

"This is strange."

"Of course it's strange, because it's an inside job."

"Like before?"

"No, not like before, Princess. It appears that was just the start. The past was a failed attempt. Whoever is truly responsible has come back ten times stronger."

Jesus.

This isn't happening.

"Don't worry your pretty little head, Persephone." He leans closer and licks over my cheek. "The only thing you need to worry about from now on is pleasing me."

"That's all you can think about?"

"Yes, especially after last night."

Fire sweeps over my cheeks at the mention of last night and I wonder how long he plans to keep me.

Lukiyan winks at me then walks back over to the desk to pick up a document that looks like a contract.

"Come here, this is for you."

"What is it?" I move closer and stop short when I see I'm right. The document is a contract.

A contract for the rights to me.

"You're making me sign a contract?" I gasp.

"I like to do things properly." He sets it down on the desk and hands me a pen. "Sign it and our agreement will be official."

I take the pen, once more thinking of my father, and sign on the dotted line.

The words blur together but I see enough to know that Lukiyan would own me completely and he wants access to my body whenever and wherever he wants.

When I straighten and look at him, his eyes roam over my body and the scandalous look he gives me, makes my entire body blush.

"Wonderful. I own you now."

"How long for? Until you get bored and throw me away?"

"We'll see about that." A sardonic smile dances on his lips.

What a fucking asshole. I can't believe I'm in this fucked up mess.

"Where is my bag? I want it." I fold my arms under my breasts and glare at him.

"You will have it back when I decide to give it to you."

"But it's my bag. Can't you stop being such a dick and give me my things?"

He catches my face, making me shudder, and I hate showing I'm afraid of him.

"That smart mouth of yours is going to get you in trouble." He taps my jaw and issues me a sinful smile.

"I just want my bag."

"And I told you, you're not getting it back until I decide to give it to you. I think it's time we go over some rules."

"Rules?" *Who the hell does he think he is?*

"Rule number one. Piss me off and I will punish you. Rule number two, defy me and I will punish you. Rule number three, if you even think of escaping, I will punish you and everybody you know in ways you will never forget. Remember the price you're paying and my kindness in accepting this agreement of ours. Is that clear, Persephone?"

Is it clear? Of course.

I can clearly see what kind of monster he is and I feel

like such a fool for the feelings I developed for him. I made terrible choices right from Brazil, and it all began when I decided it was a good idea to listen to that stupid fortune cookie.

Pretend to be someone you aren't until sunrise.

As much as my life sucked beyond measure, if I were myself, I would have run far away the moment I sensed he was dangerous.

We would never know each other and the only thing I'd feel for him now is disgust.

Not the other thing I opened my heart to when I gave him that part of me I'll never get back.

"Answer me," he prods.

"Yes. I understand."

"Good, now back to business." He releases me. "Are you on the pill?"

The question throws me, but I know where he's going with it and it infuriates me.

"Why do you need to know that?"

"Because I want to fuck you bareback. Now answer the question."

His dirty mouth zaps a stab of desire straight to my core, making my traitorous body react. As moisture beads between my thighs, I will it away, hoping to pull myself together. And my dignity.

"I have an injection," I grate out. "I got it a few weeks ago." Antonio made me get it.

"How long's it good for?"

"Three months."

"Have you been with anybody else since Brazil?"

"No." He's the only man I've ever been with and he seems satisfied to hear it. I want to ask if he's been with anyone else but stop myself. I don't want to know. I don't want to imagine him being with other women when I've spent nights fantasizing about him. But that doesn't prevent me from asking the other important question. "Have you always used a condom since Brazil?"

He chuckles. "So innocent, so pure."

"Answer the question." I sound braver than I feel.

"I'm clean."

It gives me my answer, but opens the door to make me think he's still been with other women.

It doesn't matter. I can't let that matter when there's so much to worry about.

"It's time to play with you again, Persephone. Take off your panties," he orders in a cool, measured tone, tugging on my little summer dress.

I bend down to slide my panties down my legs.

"Good girl. Now sit on the sofa and spread your legs so I can see your pussy."

Swallowing hard, I make the short trip to the sofa by the window and open my legs for him.

"Prop your legs on the seat so I can see properly." His voice becomes huskier.

I put my legs up, completely exposing myself to him. He then comes over with a smile plastered on his face.

"Pull the straps down on your dress and take out your tits."

I've never felt so humiliated and shamed in all my life, but I do as he says becoming the whore again.

Lukiyan bends down, getting between my legs and lowers to lick my pussy. I bite back a moan when the pleasure hits me.

"It's okay to want me, Persephone," he taunts when he sees I'm trying not to like what he's doing to me. "Give yourself to me."

That deep baritone sings to me like the Pied Piper's song and I fail as badly as I did last night.

Within seconds I'm reeling head over heels in pleasure and I don't want him to stop.

Briefly he pauses his feasting on my pussy to suck on my nipples then stops again with a wicked smirk curving his lips.

"Now touch yourself."

"What?" I stutter, my voice thick with arousal.

"Do it." The rough, authoritative timbre of his voice speaks directly to the need aching in my pussy, and my body yearns to obey. "Touch yourself like you do when you're alone."

Lust thickens in my throat when he guides my hands to my pussy and strokes my fingers leading me to touch myself.

I do it and it's even more arousing to have him watching me the way he is.

When I rub my clit I try to ignore the rising pleasure deep, but there's no point.

He smiles when I moan and guides me to pump my fingers in and out of my passage.

"Fucking perfect," he grates out.

I swallow hard, feeling the building orgasm already coiling in my core.

He moves back to suck my breasts while I continue my pumps, but it all suddenly becomes too much.

I come in an instant, gasping for air and he picks me up, bending me over his desk.

He rips my dress, stripping me naked then warm hands splay over my ass.

Jesus, what is this man doing to me?

I catch the reflection of us again in the glass cabinet and I don't recognize myself.

There's a look about me that appears wild and free. But how can I look free when I just signed my life away?

Lukiyan pulls off his shirt, and pushes his pants down to free his cock. Then he glides his rock hard erection over my slick opening.

I'm so wet for him he slides right into me and I suck in a sharp breath from the amazing sensation of feeling his bare cock inside me.

He's aware of it too. I can tell as he grips me tighter and presses his nose to my hair.

"Jesus, woman. You're going to ruin me."

Ruin him...

He keeps showing me glimpses of himself, but when I

want to look further he manages to maneuver me on to another path.

Like now.

He slams into my body brutally sweeping every thought of shame out of my mind. There's only the feel of him, his intoxicating scent, and his overpowering presence as he drives into me.

His cock is splitting me apart. Fracturing my mind, heart, body, and soul.

He starts fucking me harder and faster, pushing me into the desk.

I cry out in pain and pleasure as my body shatters into a million pieces and I come again.

Then it's like time stands still and we pick up where we left off last night, both of us getting lost in the insane sexual rhythm that has captured us.

After what feels like years have passed, he empties inside me, filling me with warm cum that explodes in my body, hot and intoxicating.

When his pumps slow he keeps his grasp on me and rests his chin on top of my head.

I can feel his heart pounding wildly against my back.

Turning me to face him, he cups my face in a hold that feels too sensual for him. It's too gentle.

Too intimate.

I gaze deep into his bright blue eyes and feel more exposed than I was before.

He can see me now.

All of me.

"I…"

"Shhh… don't speak, just feel. Feel me, Persephone. I am your Hades."

His mouth closes over mine and I allow myself to feel him.

What I feel is that I own him too.

He's as much my captive as I am his.

LUKIYAN

I feel like the king of the world.

In my case, I guess, the king of the underworld.

I never felt this good as a mere man. Persephone turned me into a god the moment I first touched her.

It's been two fucking weeks since we signed that agreement and we're still hyped up on the wild sexual haze that possessed us.

The sun is almost up and I'm supposed to go to work today. I just don't know how I'm going to leave her.

During this whole time, I've managed to get away under the pretense that I was splitting my time between investigating and looking for her. Instead of staying at the cottage I've also been coming straight back here because I hate being away from her.

I hate the thought of leaving her later. I hate the thought of leaving at all, but the art of making people believe lies is ensuring the lie looks legit. Which, for me, means showing my face to the man who's been looking for his daughter for a little over two weeks.

While Emilio has been worrying himself sick about his precious baby girl, we've been here fucking like animals.

The big bad wolf has been feasting on her over and over again. I've dirtied up this good girl in every way my devilish mind could conjure, and I'm about to do it again.

I currently have her gorgeous naked body sprawled out face down on my bed. Her wrists are bound with chains I looped through the headboard.

I left her feet free so she can take the hard pounding I'm going to give her ass.

But first I need this.

I take the little bag of blow next to me and pour the white powder down the line of her beautiful back and to the center of her ass.

Then I inhale the line, allowing my breath to tickle her skin.

She moans under the weight of my naked body, taking what I give her like the good sub she is. And fuck me, this girl is magic.

She must be, to have put whatever the fuck spell she put on me.

Only a spell could have changed my mind when it came to her father.

Only a spell could make me decide that taking Emilio Vittorio's remaining daughter and heir to his empire, was worse than killing the man.

The plan is very shaky because I never saw him remaining alive living in my cards.

I wanted blood for blood, but the beautiful maiden beneath me reached a place inside my soul that I thought died long ago.

I know I have to think ahead but I don't want to think about anything that's not her.

Especially not now.

Filled with the drug and the moans of the woman, my head buzzes, numbing the demons and the beast inside.

"I'm going to fuck you hard," I spank her ass and watch with raw satisfaction as her ass jiggles.

"You've been fucking me hard for the last few days," she mumbles groggily. She can barely keep her eyes open.

Sleep isn't far away and I wouldn't be surprised if she slept all day.

Neither of us has stopped.

We've both been taking and taking and taking from each other.

I've caught her trying to school herself, trying not to enjoy what I do to her as she got lost in me. I would be the same if I were her because she's not supposed to be enjoying this.

"No point stopping now. I want your ass."

I don't give her any warning; I just plunge my fingers into the tight rosette of her ass and smear the sweet nectar from her wet pussy inside.

She moans at my touch.

When I think she's good and ready for me I guide my dick to her entrance and slide right in.

Her body is now accustomed to my length and thickness but she's still so tight everywhere, especially here.

Pleasure shoots straight to my balls and I start fucking her.

I wanted to finish inside her pussy again before we call it for this session but this feels so fucking good I can't stop.

I lift her hips so I can pound into her and angle her so I can fuck her as hard as I promised. She screams when I unleash, moving faster.

It's like I've lost my damn mind.

The chains clink against the bed in tandem with our bodies slapping together and the chorus of our erotic cries.

I try to hold on for as long as possible but she feels too good. Everything about her feels too good.

From the silk of her skin to the purr of her feminine moans.

Like the villain I am, I smile when I think of how she's mine. That fucking bastard Antonio doesn't have her.

I do.

Me. Her Hades.

I took her into my dark world and claimed her in every way a man can claim a woman. And yet it feels like there's still more to take.

I come hard, blowing my cum into her passage and we both cry out one last time.

When I catch my breath, I pull out of her and she slumps back against the mattress, her body shuddering.

I release her from the chains, but she's still linked to that part of my soul.

She breathes out a ragged sigh and looks at me.

"Is this all you're going to do to me, Lukiyan? Fuck me until I die?" Her voice is barely audible.

I smile down at her. "Do you want me to?"

She stares back at me, her hair a sexy mess, her skin shimmering with her afterglow.

She doesn't need to answer, I know her.

I know what she wants.

I know what she needs.

"You mystify me, and I can't figure you out," she rasps.

Maybe it's best we keep it that way because in the real world she wouldn't be mine. The same way that darkness and light can never be together.

It's the same for me and her.

I find Emilio in Persephone's room when I arrive at work.

I have small news for him.

It won't be the news he really wants to hear though.

He's sitting on Persephone's bed looking at an album. He looks a mess. Like he's been hitting the bottle hard and seeing the bottom every time. He hasn't shaved since I was last here and doesn't look as well put together.

He lifts his head as I walk in and manages a curt nod.

"Sorry I wasn't in my office. I lost track of time," he says, waving a hand over the album.

"That's alright, Frankie said you were up here."

"Just looking at old memories I should have appreciated more." He nods. "I'm heading out to Minnesota later tonight. There was sighting of a young woman who looks like Persephone teaching ballet to some kids in the park. She taught a summer school there last year, so it could be her. I figured Minnesota is far enough to get away from here, *and me*. She also knows the place."

It would be easy to feel guilty or sorry for him if he wasn't my enemy. I should at least feel bad on some level for having him fly out to Minnesota but I don't.

He's the one who seems to have clearly ruined his relationship with his daughter. If he hadn't, he wouldn't think she needed to get away from him.

"I'll be there for a few days," he adds.

"Alright, let's hope for the best." I give him a hopeful smile, feeling like the devil I am.

He wouldn't like to know how close he came to death by my hand. In fact, every time I've seen him—including now—I've felt close to killing him.

If letting him worry himself sick about his daughter is all I can do, then I'll take it as something.

Right now, I can't help but feel I've let Melissa down in many ways, because I know deep down that I didn't just accept Persephone's offer because I found some way of still allocating blame to Emilio.

I know I accepted it for me.

Because I wanted her.

"Look at her here." He points to a picture of Persephone on stage in her ballet dress.

She's dressed as the black swan. Her leg is perfectly arched over her head in an arabesque. It almost looks unreal, like something a contortionist would do.

"That's amazing."

"I don't know if you know anything about ballet."

"I do. My mother... she um, used to do it when she was little." It feels weird talking about my family with him. "She took me and my sister to the ballet when we were younger."

"That's good. My mother did the same. That's where Persephone gets it from. When my mother saw Persephone's talent she made me promise I'd help her achieve her dream. My baby girl was fourteen in this photo."

"That's amazing." To have that type of talent at such a young age is astounding.

"It is. This is a performance she did for the National Ballet. She was the youngest dancer in the show. She got picked by a scout to play the part. We were all so proud, and she went on to do so much. So much for a person with ... the health conditions she's had."

I haven't forgotten what Persephone said about having heart surgery. I haven't asked her about it since. Every time I look at her tattoo, though, I wonder about what she must have gone through.

"What was wrong with her?"

"She had heart problems from birth. At first we

thought both girls had it but it was just Persephone. We nearly lost her a few times. Now I've lost her for good. I... look at this now and I hate myself. I might not have been able to do much about the marriage contract because we're bound in blood to fulfil the promises we make, but I could have fought for this. I could have made sure she got her dream because she was made to dance."

His words grip me because I thought the same, and I'm keeping her away from that too.

"Her sister did everything she could to help Persephone achieve her dream and I just took it away without warning." He sighs unevenly.

It's the first time he's mentioned his other daughter like this.

"Her sister?"

He shakes his head. "I... can't talk about that."

A glimmer of weakness pushes through his eyes, and I think I'm right about how Athena Vittorio died.

"I tried to do the right thing for both of them and be the leader I'm supposed to be, but I ended up ruining things. Even the small things that matter. Persephone told me she loved me and I didn't say anything back. I wanted to tell her I love her too, but things can't always be the way we want. What if she's dead, Lukiyan?"

His eyes hold mine and I feel like a bastard.

Again.

"You and I both know what the Order are like. I'm here waiting on a phone call for some ransom, or hoping she escaped this life, but the truth could just be that she's lying in a ditch somewhere. Dead. People like them killed my wife and my brother. Why wouldn't they kill my girl?"

He's right to think that. The Order are not people you can negotiate with.

"We'll keep looking." I nod, pushing away the compassion threatening to overpower me.

Anything I feel is because of her.

Persephone is doing this to me—awakening my heart. Her influence is making me feel things I don't want to feel for this man.

Because... I'm in love with her. That's the simple explanation I never wanted to admit even to myself.

I've never been in love before, but I have a penchant for spotting things with my off-the-charts attention to detail skills—even when it comes to myself.

I just didn't want to accept it.

Persephone Vittorio reached the human parts of me I work so hard to keep on a leash. Now I struggle to remember that emotions are weaknesses a man like me can't afford.

"Thank you."

"I've located some places Order members hang out. I'll be out most of the day tracking and investigating." Aleksei managed to get some information before I left.

The two of us have been working hard to find anything we can on these guys.

Emilio looks hopeful. "I should come with you."

"No, you stay here and save your energy for Minnesota. I got this covered." He looks like shit and if he's been drinking as much as I think then he'll be off his game. I don't want to have to worry about him while I'm tracking the people trying to kill him. That will be as good as serving him up on a platter.

"Okay. Take as many men as you need for back up."

"Sure." I'd prefer to work with my own team, but it would look strange if I didn't get him involved in this.

"My device will be ready on Sunday."

Does that mean he'll be seeing Judas on Sunday? "Is that when you'll be handing over to Judas Kane?" I try to sound as nonchalant as possible.

"No, he'll be in touch when he's ready to meet. I've given Frankie all the information he needs so he can take charge." His face hardens and he brings a weary hand to his head. "I want to be ready in case there's another attack. These people seem to be one step ahead of the game so I wouldn't put it past them. In all my long years, this has never happened to me, and it's made me look like an amateur at best."

"These things happen when those close to you betray you."

"I know."

"Any idea who it could be yet?"

"No." His eyes look uncertain, as if he might have thought of the answer, but isn't acknowledging it. "Promise me if anything happens to me, you'll still keep looking for Persephone."

Despite my attempt to feel nothing for him, guilt rides my shoulders when I observe the sadness in his expression. It's the kind of sadness I've witnessed before when a person is worried about death.

"Of course. I'll check in with you later."

He nods and goes right back to looking through the album.

As I walk away, I try to push aside my guilt and remember why I'm doing what I'm doing.

It's for love.

Only for love.

Who will avenge my sister if I don't?

25

LUKIYAN

My dick twitches when I reach home in the early hours of the morning and think of another wild session with Persephone.

As it's nearly two a.m., I'm sure she's asleep. As much as I want her, I won't be a bastard and wake her.

I've kept her up enough over the last few days. There's only so much sex the body can take. So I should probably take a break before my dick falls off.

I hoped to be home before now but it couldn't be helped.

If the Order members were that easy to find, I would have found them already.

I spent the day doing what I could, but didn't find anything. I'll pick up where I left off tomorrow.

The house is quiet with a blanket of silence covering it.

Apart from the guards I have milling around the property and the gentle shoosh of the waves from the sea, there's nothingness. Sometimes that's better. It beats silence.

I'm not tired so I head into my father's office, take off my jacket, and pour myself a scotch.

Father always kept the good stuff in here.

This is a thirty-year old Scotch whisky from the Kozlov cellar. It has a hint of a fruity taste that hits my tastebuds first, before the burn of the alcohol.

It numbs my mind and gives my demons some reprieve.

I'm at odds with myself, but it's only because things are still vague. Even though everything seems to be moving, nothing is really happening.

I don't have a solid plan for Judas, and I don't know what I'm doing with Persephone, or her father.

When it comes to Persephone, I know what I'm doing is wrong, but selfishness won't allow me to let her back into the light where she belongs.

If I let her go though, what will happen to her? Only the same things as before.

She'll have to marry Antonio and live with him in Italy. She'll be his.

Not mine. Not my girl.

I pour another glass of scotch to add to the numbness. I don't want to feel guilt right now and if I'm not with her, then I don't want to be aroused either.

As I put the glass to my lips and gaze out the window shock slams through me when I see the beautiful maiden walking along the beach.

She's wearing a little silk white nightdress, which flows behind her making her look like a ghost.

What the hell is she doing out there at this hour?

Setting the glass down, I open the sliding doors and walk out on to the terrace.

The chill of the cold night air ruffles my hair. She must be cold in what she's wearing, but she's walking as if she's not aware of anything.

"Persephone," I call out to her but she does nothing but keep going.

Thinking she hasn't heard me, I call her again but she does the same thing.

I know she must have heard me. When I left earlier, she wasn't in a mood with me, so I don't understand why she's ignoring me.

When I get to her and grab her arm I see why—at least I think I do.

Although her eyes are open, she has a vacant stare as if there's nothing going on in her mind.

She's sleepwalking.

She barely blinks when I catch her face and appears completely lost in whatever dream state she's in.

"Persephone wake up, Princess." I stroke her face but nothing changes. "Persephone."

"The baby. I have to get the baby," she mumbles.

"There's no baby. Let's go inside."

"The baby needs to be fed. Lilah is hungry. She's crying."

She said that as if she really believes it and I wonder if it's true.

Who had a baby though?

I tap her cheek, lightly and she seems to come to, but she looks like she's still not quite with it.

"Who's Lilah, Persephone?"

"The baby, Athena's baby. My niece. I have to find them." She looks more like herself but clearly confusion is setting in.

I feel sorry for her when she looks around frantically, trying to make sense of where she is and fright consumes her pretty face in the moonlight.

"Where am I?" She pants. "They were just here. I saw them. Didn't you see them?"

"No, Persephone you were dreaming. It was just a dream."

"It can't be. I saw them. They were in the meadow there over..." Her voice trails off as she looks ahead at the rolling waves of the sea.

She shakes her head and looks down at her chest. Then she moves away the fabric of her nightdress so she can see her tattoo.

"It's true. She's dead and she gave me her heart," she mumbles and more shock takes me when understanding forms in my mind.

The heart problems her father spoke of, the surgery she told me about, the scar.

Her father said he nearly lost her a few times.

Someone with a heart defect from birth would have needed something drastic to change if they're okay now.

Something like a heart transplant.

She gave me her heart...

She's talking about Athena. So, the heart beating in her chest is her sister's.

I want to ask her more to clarify my reasoning, but stop myself when tears spring from her eyes.

"My sister's dead," she mutters, crying harder, and all I can do is hold her.

When she grips on to my shirt like she needs me, she breaks down and her shoulders wrack as she sobs.

I was right when I suspected there were family secrets, and I feel like there's more to know about the girl I shouldn't know.

26

PERSEPHONE

The moment I open my eyes I remember what I did last night—or more specifically this morning.

It was around two a.m. when I had my stint of insanity.

This time I had one of my more powerful episodes.

My therapists used to tell me they happened because I feel guilty.

God knows how many therapists I saw, and how many different courses of treatment I had, but I'm still caught in limbo.

I was dreaming about Athena and Lilah in the meadow again and I really believed they were alive and everything was okay.

I truly believed it but when I snapped out of my reverie and saw Lukiyan's face I knew I was dreaming again. Except this time my brain couldn't handle the truth.

I ended up saying things I shouldn't have said. I think I

said just enough for him to guess there's more to me than meets the eye.

Soft piano music filters into my ears when I roll onto my side and my face brushes over the silky pillow.

I almost believe I'm imagining it then I realize I'm not. It's quiet and barely there, but I hear it because it's *Clair de Lune*—my piece.

That's what's playing. That piece holds a special place inside me and when I dance to it, I'm lost in each note. It was the piece I auditioned with for the New York City Ballet. That night, from the moment I started dancing and took a look at the judges faces I knew I'd gotten the part. As I danced I felt like the part in their new show was made for me.

Who could be playing the piano at this hour?

The sun has barely risen and the house doesn't usually seem to come alive until around eight.

Glancing at the clock I see it's five-forty five.

The music is calling to me so I grab my dressing gown, throw it on and head downstairs to the room where I saw the piano in the other day.

It was in one of the halls toward the back of the house.

The door is ajar, so I peek in and find Lukiyan sitting behind the grand piano. His fingers glide over the keys with the eloquence of a pianist who's played in

hundreds of concerts and composed even more pieces.

It's strange to see the large tattooed man with the wicked smirk and sense of style playing the piano.

Lukiyan Romanechka has his emotions under such

stringent controls that he doesn't show anybody any part of who he is unless he wants to.

What I'm seeing here is another glimpse of the man. The more I see of the man, the more the monster fades, and the more I want to stay with him.

There's already a warm smile lifting his sensual lips, it widens when he lifts his head and his eyes lock on me.

"I hope I didn't wake you." His grin turns sheepish.

"No. I was awake already and heard the music."

"Come here."

I walk over to him and he slips an arm around me, guiding me to sit beside him.

I do, snuggling against his massive muscular arm.

"I didn't know you play."

He drags in a breath. "I do sometimes. My real mother taught me how to play. She used to tell me that when she was little she'd make a wish on her birthday that she could keep going to her dance classes. She'd play this song and dance to it when she couldn't go."

That raises my interest. "Your mother was a dancer?"

"She did ballet until she was twelve, then had to give it up when her family could no longer afford lessons," he explains. "She used to take me and my sister to the ballet. This was her favorite piece."

"It's mine too. My... sister used to like it as well," I confide in him. "We used to play it while we hung out in the meadow near the house. She'd paint and I'd dance. I... feel close to her when I hear this song and I'm dancing to it, it's like doing something magical where we're still together."

I suspect he has questions after last night. Not that I'm ready to be the open book people wanted me to be after Athena died, but I don't want him to think I'm crazy.

"It's true you know," he says with a brighter smile.

"What's true?"

"The magic. Can't you feel it? My mom used to say that magic was all around us, we just have to tap into it. When you do, you find pieces of yourself you think you've lost forever."

I smile at that. It's sweet and I want to believe it. "Your mother sounds amazing."

"Thank you, she was in many ways."

I've never met anyone who was adopted speak like this about their birth mother.

"What happened to her, Lukiyan?"

"Very bad things. It wasn't just one thing that got her killed."

"Killed. Somebody killed her?"

He looks away with deep sadness in his eyes, then nods, his fingers playing over the notes of this piece that I'd christened the sad notes.

"She was a drug addict with a bad choice in men. They'd come to our home and hurt her. We lived in Russia until I was eight and we left when she got in trouble. We came here, and it was the same shit." He pauses for a moment and I wonder if he's going to tell me more.

"She met this one particular guy who was a complete

psycho. He'd beat her and beat us too. We always had social workers coming to see us, threatening to take us away. Mom would beg them and promise to do better. She'd do better for a little while, get rid of him, then he'd come back and life would be shit again. Then something happened that I never knew. The week before she died he nearly beat her to death and she took us to a foster home. She told me she loved me and asked me to remember her."

"Did you ever see her again?"

"No and I never knew that was going to be the last time." That's why he kept her name. "The next time I saw her face was on the news. They'd found her body washed up from the river. She'd been shot five times. Her killer was never found."

My soul trembles with sadness for him as I imagine what he must have gone through at that young age.

I was seventeen when I lost my mother and it felt like the world ended.

I don't know what I would have done at twelve years old, and on top of that being placed in a foster home with his sister must have been difficult too.

"I'm so sorry, Lukiyan. I'm so sorry."

"Thank you and it's okay. I guess I've had time to allow it to sink in and I got some retribution when I found her killer myself, years later."

The coldness in his voice suggests that man no longer lives, so I don't ask.

"It gave me some peace I suppose," he adds. "Although it will never bring her back."

This is the most he's ever spoken to me.

When he glances at me again, it's with openness in his eyes and I realize he's giving me an invitation to share my story. I just don't know if I'm ready, or if I can speak the words.

Or even if I should.

"You don't have to talk if you don't want to." He smiles. "I didn't share what happened to me so you would share, those dark things that eat us alive can only be spoken about when we're ready. Or with certain people."

He holds my gaze with adoring eyes.

I relax my shoulders and decide to try this—*talking*. I feel that if anyone can understand me, it will be him. "Maybe I should talk, because I'm always bottling things inside. My sister was the more talkative twin. I think you would have liked her more than me. There was nothing boring about her."

"There's nothing boring about you."

"If you'd met her, I doubt you'd think that. She had so much life in her."

"I'm sure that's true, but I know myself and I know I would have still chosen you. I don't think this is what you want to tell me though is it?"

I swallow hard and shake my head. "Do you remember what I said earlier about her? I mean when I was on the beach."

"Yes, I remember." His hands still on the keyboard as he stops playing, and he turns to face me.

I shuffle too, feeling like I might have some newfound strength to talk just from looking at him.

"I was already dying when the massacre took place. It was the start of my heart giving up on me. The doctors thought it was a miracle that it hadn't before and that I could dance the way I did. I wasn't supposed to live that long, but I did. I didn't want to die. I was on a donor list for a long time and when I went to school, I barely did anything. I think sometimes they were humoring me because of who my father is." I blink rapidly to clear my eyes. The next part is the hard part. "The day of the massacre my mother and sister locked me in the safe room. Mom was killed and Athena was taken and sold. The men who owned her raped her repeatedly. When Father found her, she was a broken mess, but she also got pregnant. She decided to keep the baby even though she was completely broken. We all supported her. All of that happened, and the thing that drove her insane was losing that baby."

"What happened to the baby?"

"She was born with the same heart defect as me. It's genetic but the kind of condition that can skip one person or a generation, even several then randomly reappear. It's on my mother's side and no one had had it since her great, grand uncle who died in his thirties. I got it, but Athena was a carrier. Her baby got it in the worse kind of way and there was nothing we could do. She died before she was a year old and that's what drove my sister crazy. She loved that baby with all her heart and she couldn't handle the loss."

My voice tracks off when my mind does and I think of that hard time I lived through.

We'd just lost mom, who would have known how to comfort us, and I was virtually dead myself.

"I took a turn for the worse and ended up in a coma. Things got so bad that my choices were a heart transplant or death. Because Athena had practically lost her mind, no one knew what she was really up to. No one knew she was about to save me. She'd gone to her lawyer and made a will just for her heart. She wanted it to go to me if she died. That night my...sister shot herself. When I woke from the coma she was gone."

The tears that fall now can't be stopped. This was the first time I'd used all those words to explain what happened.

I move my nightdress away so he can see my tattoo. "This was her last painting. Roses with blue butterflies. The scar reminded me of her death, but the tattoo reminds me of how she lived."

He pulls me into his powerful chest for a hug and I rest in his embrace which reminds me of a safe haven.

"I'm sure your sister would have loved the way you remember her."

"I just wish she was still alive."

"I know, but she lives in you, and you get to live for her."

I lift my head and gaze into his eyes. I'm still crying but I manage a smile.

"You still mystify me."

"Maybe it's better that way." He dips his head slightly.

"No."

"I think if you could figure me out, I'd be less interesting and you wouldn't like me as much."

"I think I'd like you just the same."

"Really, Persephone?"

"Yes, Hades."

27

LUKIYAN

The condition is called a progressive cardiac conduction defect. PCCD for short.

It's a rare genetic and hereditary heart rhythm disturbance condition which can lead to a complete heart blockage the heart essentially stops working.

Those with the condition must be on continuous treatment.

Those with the condition as severe as Persephone's have a shorter life expectancy.

I can completely understand why everyone was so fascinated with her because people who have the condition aren't advised to undergo strenuous exercise, let alone get accepted into Juilliard and a place with the New York City Ballet.

I stare at the computer screen showing Persephone's medical records.

These records, of course, aren't listed in her general

records. Families like the Vittorios have whatever kind of privacy they can pay for. So they can keep things secret.

But they can't hide from people like me. I've been leaving all tech-related things to Aleksei, but since this was personal I looked into it myself.

More than ever he can see my fascination with the maiden, so he would have looked into it for me, but I guess I'm not ready to talk about her yet.

Not when guilt is weighing heavily on my mind.

I've been awake for a few hours now, just sitting in my father's office. I should probably start calling it mine now since it is.

He'd want me to call it mine.

Talking about the dead yesterday weighed on me more than I showed. But sometimes you have to push aside your own feelings when others need you.

Yesterday Persephone needed me. I spent the whole day with her, and the night too.

It was nice and normal. It felt freeing in ways, but what happened to her stayed with me.

While she bared her soul to me, I wanted to look into what she went through.

That's what sent me down here before sunrise.

I've never seen medical records that look like hers before. There are pages and pages and pages in several files ranging from the time she was born, right up until years after her sister's death.

I know it was hard for her to talk about and I appreciated that she shared her bad experience with me.

I've finished looking through the files now and I feel just as awed as her doctors were that she achieved so much.

Across from me is the letter I shouldn't have read.

It's from Athena to Persephone. It reads more like a suicide note.

I saw the envelope weeks ago when I first looked through her duffle bag.

I didn't read the letter, although the envelope was already open. Reading it then would have felt like I was invading more than I already had.

Today it was calling to me as loudly as my curiosity to check her medical files.

I'm sorry I read it now because it makes me feel worse than I already do. Like I was the villain to the wrong woman.

I plan to give it back to her when she wakes up, but as I look at it again it's like her sister is speaking to me.

It says:

My sweet sister,

If you are reading this, I'm gone. I'm not alive anymore, but I am free.

I don't want you to be sad, and I don't want you to feel mad at me.

I didn't leave you because I don't love you.

Please never think that.

I did this because I could no longer live in this world without my baby girl.

Everywhere I looked I saw her. I kept hearing her calling for me, so I decided to go to her.

I made that decision and also found a way to save you.

I know you feel guilty for Mom's death, but please don't. We put you in the safe room because we both wanted you to live.

I'm doing the same thing now.

No one can dance the way you can.

It's like music was made for you.

So please accept my gift of my heart, my sweet sister and when you dance, think of me.

I am always with you.

Love always and forever,

Athena

As I read it again, I know what I must do.

I've always known what to do. But I just wanted to hold on to the one good thing that ever happened to me for a little longer.

A hurried knock on my door snaps me into focus.

"Come in," I call out.

Aleksei pushes the door open and the instant I see his

face and the Manila envelope he's carrying I know he has news for me.

"We got something. Two somethings."

"What are they?"

"Judas. I just intercepted a message to Emilio. He's going to be staying at the Grand Elk. He'll be here tomorrow at lunchtime. He's meeting Frankie on Wednesday to hand get the device."

Tomorrow.

I set the letter down, my brain processing this moment.

This is it. This is the chance I've been waiting for.

I'll get to kill that motherfucker.

"Let's get there tomorrow and kill his ass."

"My thoughts exactly. I know what room he's staying in so I'll get everything set up so we can move in."

"I need to make the kill," I cut in and he nods. "Thank you Aleksei. I couldn't have done this without you."

"Don't mention it. Ready for the other news?"

"Give it to me."

"Guess who's bestest friends with an Order member?"

He opens the envelope and takes out a picture.

When he sets it down before me and I see Antonio talking with a baldheaded guy, with the Order tattoo on his arm, I smile to myself.

"Well hell."

"Yes. What do you want to do? The street guys picked this up a few hours ago. They said he might be there again tonight, but they're not sure. The Order guys are getting a drug drop."

"Let's go there tonight. If I take him down, that means I won't have to worry about Emilio anymore."

"And what about after we get Judas?" He raises his brows. "Is the plan still to kill Emilio then?"

I know what he's asking me, and I'm going to answer because he deserves some explanation.

"I made a deal with Persephone."

He doesn't look surprised. "You care for her don't you? Don't lie to me, I'm calling rank here as your superior and your oldest friend, so give me the truth."

I smirk. As Sovientrik his authority is as powerful as the Pakhan in his absence. As my oldest friend, though, his authority is as powerful as family to me.

"Yes."

"And what are you going to do about her?"

He's asked me that question before. This time carries more weight.

"I'll cross that bridge when I get there."

We're silent for a moment then he nods. "Okay, at least it looks like we'll get what we came here for."

It does seem that way.

Now to plan and give Emilio a call. He's still in Minnesota.

I'll take great pleasure in informing him that his beloved son-in-law to be is the motherfucker who wanted him dead.

I would never have guessed Antonio was involved in

this because the fool would have gotten the empire and the seat in the council with his marriage to Persephone. But if Emilio died, he'd get all of that quicker.

Now he won't get anything.

Was he to be blamed for the past too?

Something feels off, but I guess I can clarify everything when I see him later.

I see the truth for myself. It's before me.

Antonio just walked into the clearing outside the old warehouse at the docks and joined two bulky looking men. I have the place surrounded with both my men and Emilio's.

Emilio's men don't know that my guys are here. They're on the rooftop with Aleksei. I wasn't going to go on a heist like this without my own backup. We work differently in the Yurkov to those in the Camorra.

We're like Spartans. We train as one, move as one, kill as one.

I'm hidden under the archway in the warehouse opposite the clearing.

Antonio is talking to the guy who looks like the leader.

I'm waiting for a clear shot on one of them to take Antonio in. Emilio wants him alive so he can question him then kill him himself via the Camorra methods of punishment.

He'll have his throat cut and his head severed from his

body.

His family, if found innocent in his dealings will be disgraced and exiled from the organization. If found guilty, they'll be killed by firing squad for their treachery and for the murders of loved ones past and present.

I'm here doing this, but I'm here for Persephone.

This way ensures she never has to be anywhere near this bastard ever again.

In this life or the next, because he's going to hell. I'm taking him there.

Aleksei is supposed to give me a signal then I'll move in with the team behind me.

I have a communicator in my ear waiting for it.

"I'm going to take a shot on the tall one," Aleksei says into my earpiece. He's referring to the leader. "Get ready to move."

"Believe me I'll be ready."

Seconds later, Aleksei takes the shot and the bulky man goes down.

I move in just as Antonio pulls his gun and is about to run off.

The men move in shooting at the Order members and all hell breaks loose.

When Antonio sees me coming after him, he looks like he's about to shit himself.

"Well look who the fucking rat is," I taunt firing a shot at his legs. I said I wouldn't kill him, but that doesn't mean I can't hurt him really bad or shoot off his dick the way I wanted to when he hurt Persephone.

"And you think you're the knight in fucking armor?" He jumps behind a stone pillar to shield himself.

I do the same then continue my pursuit toward him when I get a clear path.

He runs into the warehouse behind him and I follow, bounding forward as fast as I can.

I catch up with him inside, leaping through the air like a wild beast and knock him down to the ground. The dim overhead lights snap on, lighting us up as we tumble in a heap of flying fists.

He's surprisingly fast and agile. More than I thought.

Antonio manages to flip me onto my back and land two punches to my face, but I regain my composure and do the same to him. Before he can get anymore smart ideas I land a fist in his face, stunning him.

I give him another round of punches, knocking his fucking teeth down his throat.

"You motherfucker, it was you all along," I shout. "Emilio's going to kill your ass."

"Keep going Lukiyan, you know this is really about the girl," he sputters.

Yes it is. She's the main reason I'm here beating his ass.

"Keep pushing me, you stupid cunt."

"She's mine," he chokes out, through bloodied teeth. "She was always mine and I will never allow you to have her. You are scum." He has a death wish talking that kind of shit to me, but he doesn't know who I am.

His words, however, trigger memories of when people used to call me scum.

I might have been a kid and the years that passed saw my life getting better, but being pushed around by adults who should have known better is not the kind of thing you forget.

"We'll see about that," I growl.

His face becomes a bloody mess but I keep going until I hear the click-clack of the hammer cocking on a gun by my ear.

"You might want to stop, dog," comes a voice from behind me.

I stop and freeze, waiting for a chance to get myself out of this.

I never heard them coming, but then again, they could have already been in here.

Antonio could have run in here because he knew I'd be following him straight into a trap and I did it leaving my back up outside.

"Drop your weapon and get up," the man snarls.

I follow the order, dropping my weapon as I stand. I just need a moment of reprieve. Then I can teach these bastards a lesson. They'll all be dead in two minutes.

Looking over my shoulder, I find a blond man with a knife scar going across his cheek. He's aiming a Beretta at me with a wild smirk on his face. Another three men join him, training their guns on me.

Their presence gives Antonio a chance to get up.

"Hands behind your head," the blond man barks.

I lift my arms and do as he says. He taps the side of my pockets while the others come closer with their guns. The fool takes out my wallet, and I fume inwardly as he flicks it open revealing a picture of Melissa.

"Girlfriend?" he asks in a mocking tone. I don't answer him, and that pisses him off. "She looks like she'd be a good fuck." He tosses my wallet to Antonio, who catches it. I notice his face pales even through the blood and bruises I just gave him.

Something like recognition forms in his eyes, and I wonder if that's what it really is.

Did he know Melissa?

If so, have I compromised myself by having her picture in my fucking wallet?

"Interesting thing," the man behind me intones in a sing-song voice. "We noticed—"

I don't give him a chance to finish his sentence. I move so quickly and grab his gun that none of them see me coming. I flip it around and kill the asshole and his friends.

More men, however, storm the place.

Whirling around, I follow Antonio, who is hightailing it out of the warehouse and way ahead of me.

He runs through the open doors to the left and jumps onto the closest boat.

I curse myself when the motherfucker starts it up, and the engine roars to life.

He's getting away. I can't allow that to happen.

I push hard, trying to catch up with him.

I nearly do until something sharp rips through my side, and I realize I've been shot.

LUKIYAN

Aleksei and I walk into the house just before midnight.

The bullet tore through my side.

The wound is enough to keep a man in the hospital, but not me. As long as I can move, I'm walking.

I got stitches and left the hospital with pain meds, bandages, and the order to rest.

However, there's no way I can rest when fucking Antonio got away.

Apart from being a threat, he looked like he recognized Melissa from the picture. If that's the case, I could be compromised because now he'll know she meant something to me.

Even if I am compromised, I have more shit on him than he has on me and my master plan is in motion. Time is on my side and I'm hours away from killing Judas.

So I'll take the next few hours to recoup and save my strength for him.

"You alright?" Aleksei asks as I lower onto the sofa in the living room.

"Don't worry about me. I'll be good by morning."

"Just focus on Judas."

"Trust me I am."

After I kill Judas, my job is done here, but I have one *woman* who doesn't belong to me that I have to return. I just have to make sure she's safe.

That means I'm not going anywhere until I take down Antonio.

Persephone is sitting in the garden on the stone bench.

The goddess is watching over the flowers the way I imagine the mythical Persephone would—with awe and adoration.

It's nearly eight, and I have a lot planned for today. Seeing her was the first order of business.

She shuffles when she sees me and brightens when her gaze lands on the duffle bag in my hands.

"My bag."

"It's about time I gave it back to you." I hand her the bag and sit next to her.

"Thank you. I appreciate that. Are you okay? You look a little pale."

That's the least of my worries.

My side aches like a motherfucker, but I'm holding up

well. So much so that no one would ever guess that I was shot.

It's not the first time that's happened to me, and I'm sure it won't be the last.

"I'm fine." It's a lie. I'm not okay, and that's not down to my physical pains. "I have something else for you." I take out the contract she signed and hold it up.

She looks uncomfortable at the sight of it, but when I tear the document down the middle, terror washes over her face.

"What are you doing? Has something changed? Are you going to hurt my father?"

"No, I'm not. I'm not going to hurt him. I'm actually taking you back home in an hour."

Now she looks shocked. Persephone's full lips part and a wealth of confusion fills those autumn-colored eyes. "I don't understand."

"You're free. You're going home. I told your father I found you."

I called Emilio a few hours ago to let him know I found his daughter. It was a better conversation than the one we had last night about Antonio getting away.

I'd already decided yesterday that I would do this, but I was still holding on.

"Lukiyan, if I go home, I will be in the same situation. I can't marry Antonio. I can't marry him after being with you." Her eyes cling to mine with a desperation that makes me wish I could have done things differently to be with her.

Once again, she's baring her soul to me, but I don't deserve it. I never did. My decision to let her go is perhaps the first right thing I've done in years.

"You won't have to marry Antonio. He was the person responsible for trying to kill your father and the massacre in the past too."

Her mouth drops open. "What! That's ... oh my God. Really? *Antonio?*"

"Yes." I can understand her confusion. Something doesn't quite make sense, but it's not my problem. I've already identified the bad guy, and I'm only going to take him down because I don't want him to have her. The motherfucker still thinks she belongs to him. She doesn't.

"I think he wants your father dead so he can take over the empire sooner," I explain further. "Now we know what he's up to, the deal's off."

She brings her hands up to her cheeks. "I just can't believe it. It was him all along. He's the reason I lost so much. My mother, my sister, my uncle ...Maya...."

"I'm sorry. It's in hand now. Your father knows what Antonio has been up to, so he'll have his men looking for him and I will be there too. I'll help with the search to make sure you're safe"

"Thank you for doing this."

"You know you don't have to thank me for that."

"I do. I've only felt safe when I'm with you."

I brush over her cheek, thinking of the paradox we are.

What happens now, Lukiyan?" Her gaze clings to mine. "Do we go back to how we were before?"

"If all goes to plan, I should be able to get my sister's killer today. But once we find Antonio, I'm going back to L.A."

Her face pales. "L.A? So I won't see you again?"

"Persephone, I don't think we were supposed to meet, and I don't think you were ever supposed to know me. I certainly know, above everything else, that you deserve better."

"But you saved me in so many ways."

"Hades loved Persephone." I gaze deep into her eyes so she can see that I'm really trying to tell her I love her.

"Persephone loved Hades."

I bite down hard on my back teeth as her words pour over me like rich, warm honey, unlocking something more in my heart. Something I have to sacrifice too if I really love her.

"Love's not enough."

"Why? Why wouldn't it be?"

"Look what I did to you. I forced you. I wasn't your choice. If I were a good man, this wouldn't exist." I hold up the remnants of the contract and stand. "You need to go home to your father. He truly loves and misses you. And you need to dance so the world can see you and love you as much as everybody else who wanted you to dance. You know I'm right, Persephone. I'm right, and when you think of it, I'm just a different kind of monster who stole you away. I'm just choosing to do something good for once in my life."

She can't answer because everything I said is true.

"Be ready in an hour," I add, then walk away.

I wish I felt better about giving her up.

If it was such a good thing, why do I feel like I just damned my soul even more than it already is?

PERSEPHONE

I'm not sure how to feel as Lukiyan and I pull onto the grounds of the manor.

A myriad of emotions flow through me, and I can't decide which I should pick.

Yes, I'm relieved on some level, but I feel more broken than I was when I left here.

The last time I was here, Maya died, and the sound of war ripped my heart open.

Now my heart is ripped apart for other reasons that should be crazy.

On the drive here, I considered the possibility that I had Stockholm Syndrome.

But then I realized that I would have had to have fallen for my captor after he kidnapped me.

I was in love before.

I think I was in love from that night in Brazil when I first looked at him.

This man has lived in my head for over four months.

Now I'll never see him again.

We drove in silence, and now that we're here, there's so much I want to say to him, but I hold back.

Part of me knows he's right, but the other part—the fighter—wants to fight for the man she wants. So, I'm tearing up inside.

Lukiyan helps me out of the car, holding my hand, which he lets go of quickly.

That's right. I forgot. We're not lovers anymore, and to the world, we never were.

"Come on. Your father is waiting for you." Lukiyan dips his head, and I give him a small smile.

We proceed up the cobbled path leading to the front door in the same tension-filled silence.

I plan to tell my father I escaped because it's the truth. It goes without saying I'm to keep quiet about Lukiyan's true plans.

No one will ever hear anything from me.

The door flies open before we get to the steps, and Father comes out.

Except for the patch on his eye, he looks like the man he was years ago when Mom was alive.

Or when he used to love me.

Shame fills me for a few brief moments, then uncertainty. Every time I've shown him affection, he's pushed me away.

Lukiyan said my father truly loves me. I'm ashamed because I don't know if that's true. Yet as I look at Father coming toward me, I can see the love beaming from him. It's all over his face. When he reaches me, I feel it when he hugs me.

He hasn't hugged me in years, and it's been so long that I can scarcely remember how it feels to be in my father's arms.

I'd forgotten how safe it felt.

"You're home," he mutters in my ear. When he pulls away, he cups my face. "I'm sorry. I'm so sorry."

Shock flies through me. My father apologizes to no one.

"I'm sorry too. I—"

"No. There's nothing for you to apologize for."

"How about we take the reunion inside?" Frankie calls out, beckoning to us from the door with a broad smile on his face.

"I'll take that as my cue to go," Lukiyan states. "I'll be away for the day."

Father steps aside, and we both look at him.

Father thinks Lukiyan will be looking for Antonio, but only I know his actual plans for today. I worry about how I'll be once he finds Antonio and leaves for good.

"Thank you, Lukiyan." Father puts out a hand to shake his. Lukiyan gives him a firm handshake and gets back in his car.

I watch him drive away, missing being with him already.

When I look at my father, I can tell he knows I have

feelings for Lukiyan, but I don't think he will say anything about that.

"Come, let's go inside. We can talk if you want," he says.

"I'd like that. Is Raven here?"

"She'll be coming by in a little while."

"What about Alecia?" I pray she's not here.

"I sent her away while we sort out what's going on. I want to do the same for you."

I'm grateful Alecia isn't here. I couldn't stand seeing her and her fakeness, but I hope he doesn't plan to send me wherever he sent her.

We go inside the house, following Frankie into the living room.

"I should have told the maids to cook something," Frankie begins, and Father and I turn to face him.

"I can do that, brother," Father says, tapping Frankie's shoulder.

"You could, but I don't think you'll need food where you're going."

Before the confusion can even set in, Frankie pulls out his gun and shoots Father right in his stomach.

I scream as the sound of the bullet echoes through the air.

I don't get a chance to process or recover from the shock when he shoots my father again.

"No!" I scream.

Father falls to the ground and I slump to his side, holding him as he bleeds out.

"Why?" I scream, glaring at Frankie in complete disbelief. "Why would you do this?"

"It was you... all along, wasn't it?" Father stutters, his eyes fixed on Frankie. "It was you years ago and you now. I never wanted to believe it."

"That's because you're a fool."

It takes me a moment to absorb what I'm hearing. When I do, disorientation riddles my mind, along with shock and terror.

"But you got shot during the massacre years ago," I point out.

"Take a bullet, and no one will question you. It was a non-fatal wound. I had to make it look like someone came to kill us all. I should have been the only one to survive. Then I would have inherited the family seat on the council."

I understand immediately. When Lukiyan told me about Antonio earlier, something felt like it was missing because of the past.

Now I get it.

Uncle Roberto was the eldest brother.

He held the family seat on the Camorra council because it was his birthright. On his death, the inheritance jumped to my father. Because my father had daughters, our husbands would have gotten the seat once he died. Athena was older than me by five minutes, making her the eldest daughter. Her husband would have taken the seat, then her sons if she had any. If that was the case, my husband wouldn't have even been factored in for a chance, much less Frankie.

He would have had to wait a long time to get that seat, and obviously it wouldn't have happened in his lifetime.

"You should have died years ago, *Brother*, but you fucked it up." Frankie waves the gun at Father again. "You left the house, and your miserable bitch of a maid called you back. It was a pleasure killing her and long overdue."

He's talking about Maya. He killed her.

My heart seizes in my chest. I'm so disgusted, I can barely look at him.

"You came back with the cavalry to save the day," he adds. "And fucked things up for me."

"Why now?" Father asks.

He's shaking and feels cold in my arms. Blood is all over the two of us. I'm so sick of seeing blood. I've seen far too much of it spilled in my life.

I can't lose my father to death as well. Not him, not after we've been through so much. I need to get him to a hospital.

"I waited all this time because you got tight with security, and killing you is no mere task. Years ago, I had people who could help, but you killed them all. I waited for the right opportunity to present itself."

At that moment, Antonio walks in with a victorious smile. Judging from the bruises on his cheek and eyes, he looks like he's been in a fight, but triumph is beaming from within.

"You bastard." Father's voice is weaker now.

"The marriage contract gave me an ally. Antonio didn't want to wait for you to die or retire to get the empire, so I made him a deal. If he relinquished his rights to the council and gave it to me, I'd help him kill you."

Being on that council is worth more than a legion of my father's empires. Money and power are supposed to be used for the Circle and those in the alliance.

"The bonus was the device. I wanted that for myself, and you gave it to me." Frankie smiles. "We needed to get Persephone back so Antonio could get what he wanted."

"The girl and the empire," Antonio says.

"Fucking bastard," I spit.

"You'll see just how much of a bastard I can be when I fuck your brains out."

"Go to hell!"

"If that's where I'm going, I'm taking you with me." He laughs. "And your so-called bodyguard won't be able to save you."

Lukiyan. My God. He was just here. He didn't know what I was walking into.

"I know he's a fraud," Antonio adds.

"What are you talking about?" Father asks.

"Your boy is from the Bratva, and if I'm right, he came here to kill us all."

My God, this is a nightmare.

"Go, get the stuff in the office, then we'll leave," Frankie says to Antonio.

"Where are we going?" I cry.

"Somewhere far, far away."

LUKIYAN

Judas Kane is already in the hotel.

I have eyes on him on the outside, feeding me information.

I'm waiting in his suite with my men.

I've never felt more eager to kill before. My blood is simmering with the thrill of killing that bastard. The long months of waiting will be over soon. I have one shot to take him down, so I can't fail.

He'll be entering the suite with two armed bodyguards in the next few minutes. Judas is armed too, but that's not the problem if I miss the shot—which I won't.

The problem is that he'll use the guards as a decoy to get away. Then I don't know how he'll do it, but I won't see him again.

The same way people call me the Shadow, they call him the Chameleon.

Today it will be the clash of the titans, and I'm not

going down without a fight or without taking Judas with me.

The room is dark, but I'm between the bookcase and the archway leading into the bedroom. Aleksei and three of our men are in the kitchenette.

We've set things up so we can attack from all angles. From right and left, back and front.

The soft click of the lock on the main door heralds their arrival.

My heart speeds, and I place an image of Melissa in my mind.

Not her during the sad times of our lives, like when we were cold and starving in Russia with no hope of getting anything to eat or anything warmer than the tattered clothes on our backs.

I think of the times we laughed because we were truly happy. It wasn't when the Kozlovs adopted us and spoiled us rotten with whatever we wanted.

It was during the simpler times when we were with Mom, and she'd play with us in the park. That's it—simple but effective.

Those are the things that matter to me.

The door swings open, and Judas comes in first. The lights come on, and the bodyguards follow, one going to the left, the other to the right, checking the place out.

I could take the shot now, but they'd have an escape route through the door.

Once it closes, that's our time to strike. Aleksei and the others will take the guards down, and I'll deal with Judas.

I wait for the wooden door to slide across the carpet, and as it clicks shut, I raise my gun.

Bang-bang.

The gunshots rip through the air, hitting each guard in the head.

Before Judas can think to move, I shoot him straight in his chest, just a few millimeters away from his heart.

Fuck. I did it!

I got him.

I got him, Melissa. Now I'm going to make him bleed and suffer the way he made you suffer.

And I will do it with a song in my heart.

Grabbing his chest, Judas cries out in pain and falls to the floor. He tries to crawl away, but that's not going to happen.

He'll bleed out before he could get his keycard in that door.

In the Yurkov, when we want to make sure you're dead, we shoot you in the head.

When we choose the chest or the stomach, it's either a mercy killing, or we want you to die a slow death while we torture you.

Mine is the latter.

We all step out from our hiding places, and Judas' eyes go wide with terror.

He looks at me and keeps his gaze fixed on mine.

Yes. He recognizes me.

I heard he was crazy, so I'm not surprised when he

starts laughing as if his favorite standup comedian is in here doling out a series of their greatest hits.

I'm not surprised, but I don't believe he's crazy. I think he's evil.

"Lukiyan Romanechka." He says my name as if we're old friends.

"Live and in living color." Pride fills my voice, and when I smile, I know I'm the one who looks like Jack Nicholson in *The Shining*, but that's the look I'm going for.

His laugh becomes staggered as the pain takes him. From the ghostly color populating his skin, I can see that life is leaving him. However, he manages to get to the wall to rest his back against it.

"You knew I wouldn't give up until I found you," I taunt.

"I give you credit. You're the first. How... did you find me?"

"That would be my doing," Aleksei chimes in proudly.

I dip my head toward him with gratitude, then return my focus to the motherfucker I've been looking for, for what feels like millennia.

"You killed my sister, and now you'll pay." I walk up to him and shoot off his dick.

He screams with pain but ends it with another round of crazy laughter.

Maybe he is insane.

"What kind of sick motherfucker are you to kill your unborn child?" I crouch down when he starts panting, and the laughter fades.

"You don't know me. But few people do. Those who know me know I wouldn't have done that if the child was mine." He smiles wide when mine falls.

"You deny it? Melissa was pregnant with your child. I have pictures and footage of the two of you together. I also found the letters." There were love letters Melissa wrote talking about the baby and her excitement at being pregnant and in love. She called him her love.

"Those letters weren't for me." He coughs up blood and allows it to trail down the side of his mouth. "Yes, I fucked your Melissa all six ways to Sunday, but I can't have kids. If the child were mine, there's no way I would have killed her. So a job was a job."

I stare him down, holding his dark gaze, as I realize he's telling the truth.

He's already a dead man, so why lie?

"Someone hired you to kill her?"

"Yes, my avenging friend."

Damn it, there's more to this shit. "Who hired you?"

"A friend of the man she shouldn't have fallen in love with. The man she shouldn't have tricked into getting her pregnant. I was hired to get rid of her when she threatened to ruin him because he didn't want her or the baby."

"Names, give me names." I ball my hand into a tight fist.

"Knew you'd ask that. Now you just have to hope I don't die before I can tell you."

"Start talking before I butcher you." I reach for my knife and hold it up.

"Antonio Marchesi was your sister's lover, and the friend is Frankie Vittorio."

All the blood leaves my body as I stare back at him in disbelief.

What the fuck is he telling me?

Open-mouthed, I glance from him to Aleksei, then back to him. "What the fuck are you talking about? Emilio gave her to you."

"Frankie is responsible for the L.A. branch of Emilio's escort service. He recruits the poor unfortunate girls who are so desperate they'll do anything. Emilio only allocates the VIP girls to his clients and associates as he sees fit." He smiles when he sees I'm catching on to Frankie's part in all of this.

It started with him. He would have known how old Melissa was. He would have known she was an addict, and he used her.

"That's how I met her." Judas chuckles. "Frankie and Antonio are as thick as thieves. Always plotting and scheming, always fucking. Frankie cleans up Antonio's dirt. If your sister had exposed Antonio, he wouldn't be eligible to marry Emilio's daughter, and he wouldn't get the benefits of the empire." His voice is starting to sound weak. "Melissa used a fake surname. When they found out her true identity and that she was the adopted daughter of one of the Yurkov leaders, they got me to kill her and make it look like one of my *flights of fancy.* You see, no one is supposed to be able to find me. Looks like I got sloppy."

"No, you just fucked with the wrong family."

"I don't think so. I think it was them who were care-less, and Frankie couldn't scrub the dirt clean enough, so I landed in shit." His lips freeze in a smile, and the life recedes from his eyes as he dies.

I push to my feet and growl like a vicious animal.

Frankie and Antonio did this. My sister is dead because of them.

There was no way in fuck I could have foreseen this twist of shit.

But... wait.

I stare at Aleksei, who is already looking at me.

"Frankie," he mutters, and something clicks in my mind.

Things felt off with that whole scenario about Antonio and Emilio. Yes, Antonio was seen with the Order members, but it didn't all fit.

I knew the same person who tried to get to Emilio in the past had to be responsible for what's happening now.

Frankie fits.

He's the kind of man who could summon the Order and offer them whatever they want—which could be money or even the hacking device.

If Frankie and Antonio are always in cahoots, then Emilio's death would have benefited them both.

Fucking hell! I just left Persephone with Frankie.

"I have to go back to the manor," I stammer, already moving out the door.

"Right there with you." Aleksei follows.

We jump in our cars and tear out of the hotel parking lot.

I drive way over the speed limit, trying to get my car to go faster than it can.

Persephone...

God, please let her be okay.

I delivered her to the dragon himself, and placed her in the arms of danger when she was mine to protect.

Fate or coincidence...

Sometimes I believe they are one and the same, but then the Universe corrects me and shows me they aren't.

The night I met her was an example of that.

It had to be.

I refuse to believe the circumstances which led me to Persephone Vittorio could have been anything close to a coincidence.

When I first saw her, I was instantly in love.

I just never realized love had infected me until it dug its claws into my heart and ripped it from my chest, showing living proof that I'm still human.

At that moment, I understood perfectly why Hades did what he did.

So when my Persephone danced her way into my life, I decided she had to be mine, no matter the cost.

No matter the sacrifice.

No matter that stealing her from the light meant pulling her into my world of , death and darkness.

She was always going to be mine to keep.

Mine always.

Mine, whether she wanted to be or not....

So I can't let her go.

I have to save her and love her and keep her away from the darkness.

When we drive onto the manor and the guard at the gate, who I'm used to working with, opens fire at me, I get my confirmation that I've landed in the heart of trouble.

And clearly, they know now that I'm not who I said I was.

PERSEPHONE

"I'm sorry, my sweet girl," Father mumbles, squeezing my hand.

"There's nothing to be sorry for." I wipe the cold sweat from his brow.

He's still lying on the floor in the living room. I have his head cradled against my lap.

We've been here for over an hour now, and he's getting worse.

When Frankie left us, I managed to grab a few cushions to make Father more comfortable. I also used one to apply pressure to his wound. It's now soaked with his blood.

"My heart is filled with sorrow for everything." He coughs. "I'm sorry about Frankie too, my love. I know how you loved him. He was your favorite uncle. My little brother."

Frankie...

I still can't believe this is happening or that he's the same person I looked up to—my *cool* uncle. I can't comprehend how Frankie could be this evil person who's taken so much from my family and me.

Everything he did had a destructive domino effect, with one bad thing fueling another.

When I think back to the massacre, I feel sick.

And those men who took Athena and raped her? That was his doing too.

All the good he did was just a pretense of shit with no real meaning.

"There are no words Father," I mutter.

"I know. There are no words for how I treated you either." Father's voice is faint. I'm so scared he will lose consciousness and be gone forever. "I felt that I lost Athena because I was so worried about saving you that I couldn't see how broken she was or that she needed me. Losing her and your mother was too much. Much too much. I didn't know how to love you after because the grief hurt so badly."

"I understand."

"Then you're a better woman than I raised you up to be, and I'm so proud of you. I called Juilliard, and they want you back if you do some makeup classes."

"Oh, Father."

"And that means you'll keep your place with the New York City Ballet. I pray you get to dance again and live your dream. I wish I could see you, but I won't."

"Don't talk like that, please. I need you."

"You never needed me. You were always stronger than you thought you were. That's why you are called Persephone. It was me who named you, and your mother agreed it suited our brave little girl."

"I didn't know that."

"Now you do. Persephone, Goddess of Spring. A time when everything is reborn and given new life. I prayed you would live, and you did. *Amore mia*, I love you."

The door crashes open, and Frankie comes in with Antonio.

"Get her up. It's time to go," Frankie orders.

"I'm not leaving my father."

"Foolish girl, don't you see he's on the verge of death. He's dying as slowly as I wanted him to. So he can watch as he loses everything, including his life."

I look back at Father and see how much weaker he looks now in just the mere seconds that have passed.

Antonio marches up to us and grabs my arm, yanking me up so hard my shoulder feels dislocated.

Father winces as his head slips off my lap.

"Let me go!"

"Shut the fuck up and come," Antonio snarls, dragging me away.

Just then, the sound of gunfire booms from outside, and we stop.

The double doors ahead crash open, slamming into the walls on either side, and Lukiyan walks in with his gun aimed at Frankie.

My heart leaps into my throat at the sight of him. I can't believe he came back.

How did he figure everything out or that I was in trouble? It doesn't matter. He's here now.

Lukiyan cuts me a glance which provides a fleeting moment of reprieve I was desperate for.

However, any comfort I feel is extinguished when Frankie aims his gun at Lukiyan.

The sadistic smile on Frankie's face gives more of an insight into the monster he is.

"Back so soon, Lukiyan?" Frankie taunts.

"Cut the shit. I know what you did." Lukiyan looks at Frankie and then Antonio. "I know what you did too."

I get the feeling he's not talking about what either of them did to my family.

He's talking about something else. Since I've only seen that murderous look in his eyes when he spoke about his sister, I can only assume it's to do with her.

Frankie and Antonio did something to her.

"Lukiyan Romanechka. Is that even your real name?" Frankie smiles.

"It certainly is."

"Who was Melissa Kozlov to you?"

"My sister."

"Oh, so this is big brother's revenge. Did you know your sister used to suck my cock and let me fuck her to get money for her next fix?"

My stomach churns, and bile rises in my throat.

Lukiyan looks ready to kill, but I can see the situation here.

They're both pointing guns at each other, Antonio has me, and my father is in the corner. When bullets start flying, one or more of us will die.

Lukiyan's not retaliating yet because I'm right in the middle of it.

"I suppose you happily obliged," Lukiyan spits.

"I did what I could. She was a pretty girl."

"What about you, Antonio?" Lukiyan's gaze hardens when he looks at Antonio. "You knew she was pregnant with your child, and you got the psycho to kill her?"

Oh my God. The baby was Antonio's.

As raw mortification sweeps over me, I glance up at Antonio. He flicks his eyes down to me, but his flinty gaze doesn't change.

"I did. Shame about her crazy ideas. She was a good fuck until she thought she could trick me. But she probably did that because she was raised in the Bratva. You tried to trick us all too, didn't you? You made us think you were a simple guard."

The floorboards creak and footsteps sound in the room to the right. The guards working for Frankie come into view, and their presence is just the right distraction for Lukiyan when they start firing at him.

Lukiyan doesn't allow them to faze him. He cocks the hammer on his gun, and the bullet that flies out of it when he fires hits Frankie straight in the head.

Frankie falls to the ground instantly with his eyes wide and unmoving. *Dead.*

"Come!" Antonio shouts, pulling me along.

I try to get away from him, but he's too strong. I'm little more than a ragdoll as he drags me away.

As the gunfire continues, I look over my shoulder.

Aleksei and some other Bratva guys have run in and are shooting at the guards.

Lukiyan gets shot, and I scream.

That's the last thing I see before Antonio pulls me through the doors.

"Get your hands off me!" I shout.

"You are mine, Persephone. Mine. I'm the one who loves you."

I could almost laugh. "You don't know the first thing about love."

"Shut the fuck up. You don't know what you're talking about. We're supposed to be together, so he can't have you."

I can't go with him. I can't allow him to take me.

When we get out into the garden, I yank my arm again. He tugs back, and at that moment, I catch a glimpse of his gun in his jacket pocket.

Without a second thought, I reach for it and shoot him in his side before he can register that I have his gun.

He shouts in pain, releasing me as he grabs his side. "You little bitch."

I shoot him again near the same spot. "That's for hurting me. I fucking hate you!"

I thought he was going to fall, but instead, he growls and lunges for me.

I try to run away, but he manages to grab my arm and backhands me across my face so hard that I fall to the ground.

I drop the gun but try to reach for it again when he comes after me.

Just as he lowers, a bullet lodges in the side of his head.

Another pierces his neck.

I turn around to see Lukiyan standing across from us, getting ready to shoot Antonio again.

Antonio is already dead before he hits the ground, but when Lukiyan reaches us, he shoots him five more times, leaving his head in a bloody mess of stomach-churning gore.

Lukiyan only stops because he's run out of bullets.

He looks at me with his blood-splashed face, drops the gun, and rushes to my side.

Blood runs down his arm from his injury, but he scoops me up and holds me.

"You're safe now. You're safe with me." He presses his lips to my ear, then cups my face. "I will never let anyone hurt you ever again."

"Oh, Lukiyan." I brush my nose against his.

"Come. Let's get your father to the hospital. This isn't over yet."

It's not because my father could still die.

32

LUKIYAN

I needed surgery this time to get the bullet out of my shoulder.

It was nothing compared to what Emilio went through.

By the time the paramedics arrived, we had actually lost him. His heart stopped beating, and they came in while I was performing CPR.

It was only with their defibrillator that they brought him back, but he remained in a coma.

He had surgery and came out of the coma two days ago but was still in and out of sleep.

Today is the first he's looked alive and more like himself.

I've just come back to the hospital after getting Persephone some real coffee, and I was told Emilio was asking for me.

I expected to see Persephone in his room, but she isn't.

Emilio looks at me when I walk in, and the color returns to his face.

In the moments when he's been alert, he's seen me taking care of his daughter.

He's also had people come by from his office, so I'm sure he must know Judas is dead, and I'm sure he knows I killed him.

I don't know if that's why he wants to see me, but I'm here.

I don't know how I feel about him and his part in Melissa's death—because in my head, he still played a part —but I'm here.

I don't know if I still feel like killing him, but I'm here.

Moving to the nightstand, I set the Styrofoam cup of coffee down and go over to Emilio's bedside.

"I thought you might not come," he mutters in a weak voice, which is so unlike him.

"Why?"

"Because I wanted to see you, and she didn't ask you first."

"I'm here. How are you feeling?"

He presses his lips together. "Like hell, but I'm here too. I didn't die, and I don't take that lightly. Not every-body gets a third chance to live. I did."

"I guess that makes you lucky."

"Or, you more compassionate than you should be."

I keep my gaze on him, on the milky white eye and the good one. Emotion sparks, reminding me of the look of hope Persephone sometimes has.

I recall him saying she's like him. He couldn't have been more right.

"You think I'm compassionate?"

"You know you are. There were many things you did that you didn't have to do. This is one of them. Thank you for what you did, Lukiyan. I'm truly sorry about what happened to your sister." He pauses for a moment on seeing the clench in my jaw but continues. "Her death was a gross error on my part. I accept the blame. I gave her to Judas, and that's where everything else went wrong. I'm sorry."

Hearing his apology should mean nothing to me, but it takes the edge off my heartache and heals me in some ways.

"We're good here," I say, stopping him from continuing. "I will always harbor resentment in my heart because I couldn't save my sister, but I have to move past this if I want to be with Persephone. I love her, and she loves you, so I have to find a way."

He stares at me for a few moments and swallows hard. "You're her Hades."

"Yes."

"Please don't keep her away from the light."

"I won't."

He smiles. "Does this mean you'll be staying in New York?"

"I can be anywhere I want to be." I've already thought ahead and made my decision. I don't need to be in L.A. to do my work for the Yurkov. Even so, I would still choose her. "So where she goes, I follow, and I'm not going anywhere without her. She's… my something good."

"That's good to know. She looks happy to hear that too." He looks over my shoulder with a broad smile, and I follow his gaze.

Persephone is standing in the doorway, watching us with the brightest smile on her face.

She rushes over to me, and I take her into my arms, savoring the feel of her and finding my light.

My true love.

My Persephone.

EPILOGUE

PERSEPHONE

Sao Paulo, Brazil
Six months later

"I'm going to fuck you," my handsome husband husks in my ear in that deep baritone that has continued to bewitch me.

"I know you are."

The thought of him ripping off my clothes and fucking me right here against this wall makes my head spin and my pussy clench with need.

His lips crush against mine, sending explosive waves of pleasure through me.

I can't believe we did this.

We eloped to Brazil yesterday and took our vows on the beach this morning.

We've spent every minute since in this house, in this bedroom where we first lost ourselves earlier this year.

Our actual wedding isn't set for another six months, but we couldn't help ourselves.

Raven is going to kill me when she finds out what I did. She's planned two weddings for me now, and she never got to see me walk down the aisle.

I'm sure when she's finished with me, Father will either skin me alive or be happy for me because he keeps hinting at grandkids.

Lukiyan and I had to do this, for us.

It's precisely the kind of wild and reckless idea that suits us. And we timed it perfectly, too.

I graduated from Juilliard and I've started working with the New York City Ballet. My first performance will be at Christmas.

This wedding was the breath of fresh air I needed.

Altogether, everything feels like I've been pumped with new life and energy, and it all began with this man.

He gives my lips a punishing kiss and rips off my clothes the way he did the first time we were together.

Catching my wrists, he wraps a silk tie around them and binds my hands over my head.

"You're mine, Mrs. Romanechka. My Persephone." His voice whispers over my skin, hot and raw, stirring every part of me to life.

"And you're mine, Mr. Romanechka. My Hades."

"Always and I love you."

"I love you too."

Pulling down my lower lip, he places some beads of pomegranate in to my mouth and we laugh. He then lifts my leg and slides his cock into my slick opening, and I close my eyes as he takes me out of this world where I'll always live my dreams. Because he is my dream.

LUKIYAN

L.A., California

I walk across the lush green grass to my sister's grave.

Melissa is buried next to my adopted parents. They have a private family plot that looks more like a garden.

It has a lake running around it, and the scenery is beautiful.

When I get to the graves, I give my parents a red rose each, crouch down at Melissa's, and place a white lily on hers.

Lilies were her favorite.

I run a finger over a patch of dirt and make a heart the way we used to when we were kids playing in the park.

I've been here several times since I killed the men responsible for her death.

This is the first time I've come here and felt at peace.

"Melissa, I'm okay now." I am. "You don't have to worry about me anymore. The demons are gone and I have the light back in my life. Thank you for being you. I will always love you."

Persephone danced into my dark world and guided me back to the world of the living.

Loving her made me free.

THANKS SO MUCH FOR READING.
I HOPE YOU LOVED LUKIYAN AND PERSEPHONE'S STORY.
TO DIVE IN TO MY DARK SYNDICATE WORLD OF SEXY MAFIA
MEN START WITH RUTHLESS PRINCE.

OR JUMP STRAIGHT INTO THE BLOOD AND THORNS DUET TO
READ LUCCA AND ARIA'S STORY.

Lucca was featured in Deadly Games as Lukiyan's Pakhan.

Aleksei is also in this duet. He will be getting his own story very soon.

Thanks again xx

Deal with the Beast

Theirs

ACKNOWLEDGMENTS

For my readers.
Always for you.
Thank you for reading my stories.
I hope you continue to enjoy my wild adventures xx

ABOUT THE AUTHOR

Faith Summers is the Dark Contemporary Romance pen name of USA Today Bestselling Author, Khardine Gray. Warning !! Expect wild romance stories of the scorching hot variety and deliciously dark romance with the kind of alpha male bad boys best reserved for your fantasies. Dive in and enjoy her naughty page-turners.